The Walk-In

Amar Bhushan joined the Indian Police Service in 1967 and was assigned to Madhya Pradesh. For seven years, he dealt with crime and law and order problems but remained a reluctant policeman. When the opportunity for working in intelligence organizations came, he grabbed it and never looked back till he retired as the chief of India's foremost technical intelligence agency. He began the second innings of his career by briefly serving in the BSF intelligence, State Special Branch and Intelligence Bureau and ended up working in the Research and Analysis Wing for the next twenty-four years.

His published work, *Escape to Nowhere*, remained on bestseller lists for eleven weeks. He lives with his wife and daughter in Bangalore but seldom misses an opportunity to visit his granddaughters in the US and his mother in Jasidih, a village in Jharkhand. His previous book, *The Zero-Cost Mission/The Wily Agent*, was published in 2018 as first part of The Spymaster Series, to rave reviews.

Anne Morrow [illegible] married [illegible]

[illegible]

[illegible] was published [illegible]

The Walk-In

Amar Bhushan

HarperCollins *Publishers* India

First published in India by
HarperCollins *Publishers* in 2019

Building 10, Tower A, 4th Floor, DLF Cyber City, Phase II,
Gurugram Haryana – 122002, India
www.harpercollins.co.in

2 4 6 8 10 9 7 5 3 1

P-ISBN: 978-93-5357-013-2
E-ISBN: 978-93-5357-014-9

Typeset in 10.7/13.6 Cardo at
Manipal Digital Systems, Manipal

Printed and bound at
MicroPrints India, New Delhi

To Putool, my sister-in-law and my truly original admirer who genuinely enjoyed reading every word that I wrote and made me read to her my remaining unpublished operational stories as she began losing her battle to amyotrophic lateral sclerosis

The Walk-In

Dhaka, 1994

Life in Dhaka had come to a standstill. The streets were deserted and except for the police patrols moving around the city in their rickety vans, all other means of transport remained anchored to their stands. Shutters of shops were down and there was no sign that even kiosks selling tea and daily utilities would open before afternoon. Surprisingly, the workers of the League, the main opposition political party, who had called for a half-day strike to demand the dissolution of the parliament followed by fresh elections held under a neutral caretaker government, were nowhere to be seen. But such was the fear of the League that none dared defy their call; even daily wage earners chose to stay indoors.

Since the Indian High Commission was also closed till 2.00 p.m., Jeevnathan, the head of India's external intelligence agency unit in Dhaka, woke up late, had a leisurely breakfast and went to the study to dispose of pending papers. At 11.00 a.m., Mukul walked down from the High Commission to hand over an urgent cable to Jeevnathan. Mukul was an attaché in the crypto section of the Agency, which functioned 24x7, unaffected by holidays, natural calamities and the agitations organized frequently by political parties. This section was the only means of transmitting secure communication in troubled times, the other being landline phones, which were routinely bugged by the local counter intelligence units.

The cable was from Ashish Roy, the desk officer for Bangladesh at headquarters in Delhi. He wrote that the assessment of the source 'PY' on the gains of the recently concluded visit of the Bangladeshi prime minister to Beijing was 'highly speculative' and did not gel with reports from other independent assets. Jeev, as he was known to most, took the comments with equanimity. Ashish usually ran down his reports, for he believed that no one in the Agency read the pulse of Dhaka better than him. Born in Bangladesh, but raised in India following the Partition in 1947, Ashish had evolved over the years into a complex Bangladesh watcher, perennially torn between the pangs suffered during the Partition and an abiding longing for his erstwhile motherland. This not only clouded his objectivity but also gave him a false sense of expertise about the lives and choices of Bangladeshis and their political, social, economic, religious and cultural responses to events around them.

Jeev returned the cable to Mukul and asked him to hand it to his secretary. After Mukul left, Jeev walked out to the sprawling back garden to see what Manini was doing. She was watering the roses, which were in full bloom, swaying gently in the cool breeze. To lend her a hand, he picked up the secateurs to clip the wild growth around a few of the rose bushes, only to hear Manini scold him.

'The doctor has warned you not to bend. It will aggravate your backache. Go and sit in the shade. I will join you soon,' she commanded.

Jeev returned the pruning shears to the toolbox and waited idly for ten minutes, watching her instruct the gardener. He soon grew restless, however, and returned to the study, collected his papers, put them in his briefcase and went upstairs to get ready. From the balcony outside their bedroom, he saw that life had slowly begun to return to the streets. Rickshaws, the unmistakable symbol of Dhaka's traffic, had started plying, threatening to gradually take over the roads. The famous sweet shop in front of their house, owned by a Hindu, had already opened. The shopkeeper had remained in Dhaka despite losing most of his family members in the liberation war of 1971.

Around 1.30 p.m., Jeev had lunch, after which he called his secretary to check whether all officers had reported to the office. At 3.00 p.m., he drove to the office, navigating his way through the chaotic traffic. By then, Dhaka was back to its usual hustle-bustle.

Soon after he settled down, Jeev, who had also been assigned to the High Commission to look after consular work, was told by his deputy that the officers were having a tough time coping with the sudden surge in visa applicants. Many of them had been waiting outside the High Commission since early that morning and were demanding the urgent clearance of their cases as they had booked their flights to India for that very evening. The line of applicants was growing every minute. As the morning hours had been lost to the hartal, only emergency cases were being entertained, the deputy explained, but even that number was sizeable. He wondered if he could forward some cases to Jeev to review and interview, and decide whether they could be cleared without complying with standard verification procedures. Jeev agreed.

Within five minutes, the deputy returned with a stack of applications. Jeev had a cursory look through them and asked his secretary to start sending in the applicants, one by one.

It was 6.00 p.m., one hour past the official closing time of the High Commission, when the last visitor walked in. He was fairly tall, thinly built, of light brown complexion and sported an untamed beard. He was young, probably in his late twenties. He wore dark sunglasses and his thick black hair hung loosely to his shoulders. In his tight-fitting dark blue trousers and green bush-shirt, he looked every bit the roadside Romeo. Jeev was completely put off by his appearance.

'I have gone through your application. Your case cannot be cleared without Delhi's approval,' he said tersely as the applicant pulled up a chair, took off his sunglasses and sat down without waiting to be asked to sit. Jeev thought he was crude and aggressive and certainly not the type who would be invited to India to attend a Tablighi Jamaat, a religious congregation.

'I did not come here to obtain a visa,' the young man declared. 'I used the application form to gain entry into the High Commission and deliberately put down a dubious-sounding reason for the purpose of my visit so that I could meet you. I have no interest in going to India for Tablighi work,' he said blandly.

'Then what are you here for?' Jeev questioned him sharply.

'I want to help you in your operations and source work,' the man replied confidently, taking Jeev completely by surprise.

'Are you sure you have come to meet the right person in the High Commission?' Jeev asked.

'Yes,' the visitor affirmed.

Used to being addressed as 'sir', Jeev found the missing honorific to be rude.

'I don't think you have. I deal only with consular matters. I am not aware if anyone in the High Commission handles intelligence work,' Jeev tried to put him off.

'I know who you are and what you do here. I had earlier approached Mr Bijon Mukherjee, one of your field operatives, to arrange a meeting with you, but he was scared of talking to you about me. Maybe he wanted me to work as his source. He would often ask why I wanted to meet you, but I easily sidestepped his queries. Today I decided to take a chance and here I am,' the young man announced bravely.

Jeev was annoyed that Bijon had not informed him about this person, nor did he recall seeing any reference to him in the list of Bijon's newly raised contacts. What mystified Jeev was the visitor's audacity in revealing his intent so blatantly. He surmised that the visitor was a plant, sent over by the Inter-Services Intelligence (ISI) of Pakistan, or the Directorate General of Forces Intelligence (DGFI) or the National Security Intelligence (NSI) of Bangladesh, either jointly or separately, as part of a plan to infiltrate his set-up. He therefore decided to keep his interaction brief, vague and formal. His initial reaction had been to dismiss the young man outright, but the fact that he knew so much about Jeev's real work forced him to play along cautiously. He was, however, determined not to encourage the visitor to entertain fanciful ideas of working for him to carry out intelligence operations.

'If I need any help, I will certainly ask for you,' Jeev said politely. 'You can leave your number and address,' he suggested.

'My name is Anwar,' the man declared and took out a piece of paper from the back pocket of his trousers. It seemed he was in no mood to leave in a hurry. 'This has my address and telephone numbers,' he said and passed Jeev the slip.

'Thanks.'

'You will not share these numbers with anyone, not even with Mr Mukherjee,' Anwar dictated. 'I may not answer the call if you ring up one of these numbers but someone will. Ask for Lateef. That is my real name. The person who answers may ask where you are calling from. Tell him that you are calling from Ajmer Sharif. I will come to meet you four days after receiving your call. Trust me, I can be very useful to you,' he assured Jeev, who was amused by the young man's cockiness.

'So Lateef is your real name?' he asked.

'I use two names. Lateef is for my friends. But you should enlist me as Anwar in your records. In your language, it will be my nom-de-plume,' he said.

Jeev was yet again taken aback by Anwar's audacity. It was evident he was a crook and a dangerous peddler of information, but Jeev could not brush him aside easily.

'I have to leave to accompany the High Commissioner for a meeting at the foreign office,' Jeev said to cut the conversation short. 'I will contact you soon,' he said as he stood up and walked across the room, opened an almirah and took out a file. Then he buzzed his secretary to tell him to come in to secure the room before leaving. But Anwar was not ready to leave.

'Since I have access to the Pakistani High Commission and I am friendly with two of their ISI officers, I will be able to inform you in advance where they are training Indian

Inside Nepal

Amar Bhushan joined the Indian Police Service in 1967 and was assigned to Madhya Pradesh. For seven years, he dealt with crime and law and order problems but remained a reluctant policeman. When the opportunity for working in intelligence organizations came, he grabbed it and never looked back till he retired as the chief of India's foremost technical intelligence agency. He began the second innings of his career by briefly serving in the BSF intelligence, State Special Branch and Intelligence Bureau and ended up working in the Research and Analysis Wing for the next twenty-four years.

His published work, *Escape to Nowhere*, remained on bestseller lists for eleven weeks. He lives with his wife and daughter in Bangalore but seldom misses an opportunity to visit his granddaughters in the US and his mother in Jasidih, a village in Jharkhand. His previous book, *The Zero-Cost Mission/The Wily Agent*, was published in 2018 as first part of The Spymaster Series, to rave reviews.

Inside Nepal

Amar Bhushan

HarperCollins *Publishers* India

First published in India by
HarperCollins *Publishers* in 2019

HarperCollins Publishers India, Cyber City, Building 10-A, Gurugram, Haryana-122002, India

www.harpercollins.co.in

2 4 6 8 10 9 7 5 3 1

P-ISBN: 978-93-5357-013-2
E-ISBN: 978-93-5357-014-9

Typeset in 10.7/13.6 Cardo at
Manipal Digital Systems, Manipal

Printed and bound at
MicroPrints India, New Delhi

MIX
Paper
FSC
FSC® C218906

This product is made of FSC®-certified and other controlled material.

HarperCollins Publishers, Macken House, 39/40 Mayor Street Upper, Dublin 1, D01 C9W8, Ireland

Acknowledgements

I owe this book to Mr Vishal Bhardwaj, the extraordinary film-maker and Shantanu Ray Chaudhuri, former editor at HarperCollins India. But for their prodigious indulgence, these intelligence missions would have remained untold and buried in my dusty papers.

Vishalji, as I endearingly call him, was the first to read these stories. Since he found them immensely readable and helpful in unravelling the complexity, tragedy and joy of undertaking covert operations, he persuaded Shantanu to go through the script. Shantanu was equally excited but he did not have it easy to sell the idea of publishing spy tales based largely on live operations and expressed as a work of fiction, to his colleagues. However, once the deck was cleared, there was no stopping him. He began by lending invaluable suggestions to flesh out the original stories to make it more illustrative of individuals and times in which these operations were conceived and carried out. Then, he harnessed Shreya Dhawan's editing acumen to ensure that the narrative remained concise, free flowing and devoid of technical jargons. In the final stages of the book, Rea Mukherjee, assistant editor, HarperCollins, pitched in to make certain that the stories sparkled with all edges softened and Shantanu's absence did not affect more intelligence operations to see the light of the day. I am immensely thankful to all of them.

My loving daughters also deserve a pat on their back – Keshani, for always providing a fresh perspective on how to script the events and Nilyanka, for making sure that I have the right environment to take pleasure in writing.

Inside Nepal

Lucknow, 1989-90

The phone was ringing insistently in the living room. Before Jeevnathan, head of the Eastern Service Bureau (ESB) of India's external intelligence agency, could get out of bed to answer the call, it stopped ringing. Groggily, he looked at the bedside clock. It was 5.30 a.m. He wondered who it could have been. Perhaps it was his wife, Manini, calling from Delhi. Jeevnathan, popularly known in the Agency as Jeev, had recently returned to India after completing a foreign assignment to take up his new post at the ESB. Till such time as he rented proper accommodation in Lucknow, Manini was staying in Delhi with the kids in a guest house, attended to by a disgruntled caretaker. Was something wrong? He began to worry. It was very early for her to be calling. He was about to get out of bed to call her, when the phone shrieked again. Jeev hastily threw off the quilt and drew aside the curtain to check if daylight had broken. It was still very dark outside and drizzling. For the last ten days, Lucknow had been reeling under a severe cold spell, made worse by frequent rains. Jeev shivered and threw a shawl around his shoulders before hurrying to the living room. But by the time he reached the phone, it had stopped ringing. Becoming increasingly worried, he wasted no time in booking a lightning call to Manini. During the eighties and early nineties, the telecommunication services in India were basic at best. The only service provider was the state-controlled Post and Telegraph Department, which provided landline phones, supported by a poor network and outdated equipment and manned by indifferent employees. Long-distance calls had to be booked through an operator, and were prioritized as ordinary, urgent, immediate, most immediate and lightning. Accordingly, operators planned their response time to connect calls. It was a different matter that in most cases, calls never materialized.

Jeev brought a pillow from the bedroom, pulled the phone closer to him on the coffee table and lay down on the sofa. He cursed his rule-bound accountant who would not permit him to buy a cordless device or a phone with caller identification simply because it cost fifty rupees more than his financial powers allowed him to sanction. He struggled for a while to stay awake but soon fell asleep. He had returned to the safehouse where he was staying at around 1.00 a.m. from a failed visit to meet one of his predecessor's sources on the border. He had made the trip in a rickety Willy's jeep and was exhausted. He woke up with a start when the phone began shrilling again. He rubbed his eyes, sat up and reached for the receiver, hoping that the lightning call to his wife had come through. But the caller was Naveen Sharma, the desk officer of Nepal operations at headquarters and a friend of Jeevnathan's.

'I have been trying to reach you since early this morning but you didn't pick up the phone,' Naveen complained.

'Why, is there a crisis?' Jeev enquired.

'You could say that,' Naveen said. 'Yesterday, the Chief decided in a meeting to shut down the Eastern Service Bureau with immediate effect and directed me to communicate this to you.' Naveen hesitated before continuing, 'I'm sorry. I know you just moved to Lucknow and another transfer within weeks of your arrival will be hard, especially since you just rented a house and Manini and the kids will be joining you in the next few days.'

Not quite believing what he was hearing, Jeev asked, 'Are you going to shut down the Eastern Service Bureau for good?'

'Yes. The plan is to withdraw ninety-five per cent of the employees of the bureau, including you, following the closure of all the units dotted along the border,' Naveen briefed him. 'All unproductive operations that are being run by your station are to be scrapped. All field operatives are to suspend their source work and fix no further meetings with their assets. A team of two or maximum three personnel under a junior officer will, however, remain in Lucknow. Their job will basically be to liaise with the government of UP and its intelligence agencies. A review of this skeleton unit's usefulness will be undertaken after six months,' he added.

'What suddenly provoked you to take this quixotic decision to shut down the bureau?' Jeev asked in anger.

'It isn't as sudden or quixotic as it seems,' Naveen replied. 'Over the years,' he explained, 'we have been monitoring the ESB's performance and have found its output, both in terms of quality and quantity, to be steadily declining. Though a large number of sources are being run, the usable value of their reports has been poor and not worth a rupee. Similarly, the station's current operations are being run around insignificant targets and produce unreliable inputs. To make matters worse, the reports from sources often reach headquarters long after the events have taken place and therefore cannot be shared with the concerned government departments. I have compiled seven years of statistics to substantiate these findings, which I gave to the Chief, but I refrained from suggesting any course of action,' he added.

'Was Rajan present in the meeting?' Jeev asked.

'Yes. He endorsed my views, pointing out that under the circumstances, we could not justify maintaining such a huge bureau with hundreds of field operatives and administrative staff, when more important operational commitments were suffering due to a shortage of manpower. The Chief agreed and directed me to ask you to submit a report within a fortnight, outlining the phase-wise withdrawal of your bordering units. Separately, Rajan wants you to make a quick assessment of your financial and logistical requirements and send it to us at the earliest,' Naveen said.

'So, it's you who have been working to consign the ESB to the dustbin of the Agency's history,' Jeev said acidly.

'You are not being fair to me. I could not be a mute spectator to non-performance of this magnitude,' Naveen defended himself.

'I can understand your sense of outrage over the functioning of the ESB, but what I do not appreciate about this decision is that I was kept completely in the dark about this possibility. No one at headquarters, not even you, gave me the slightest hint that I was being assigned to the ESB only for a few months and that too for shutting it down,' Jeev complained.

'Please don't misunderstand me, Jeev. It was never my intention to put you in such an awkward position. We have been friends for years and you know how much I lobbied to keep you in Delhi. Believe me, neither I nor Rajan has played Brutus to you.'

When Jeev said nothing, Naveen continued. 'My task was limited to carrying out an objective review of the ESB's work and submitting it to the Chief. I handed it in to him some six months ago, but heard nothing from him thereafter. It was only yesterday that he finally announced his decision. Since we were not sure what view he would finally take, I avoided mentioning anything to you,' he explained.

Jeev was unconvinced.

'You may have your reasons, but I wish you had been more straightforward with me. You could have at least mentioned the poor state of source work at this unit and your expectations from me. In hindsight, I can see where I misjudged the signals. When I went to call on the Chief on the day I was leaving for Lucknow, he smugly told me to enjoy my new assignment and to make the most of my time in Lucknow. I didn't realize that he was actually being sarcastic and deliberately waylaying me so that I did not object to my posting to Lucknow for a few months,' Jeev said. 'Anyway, it seems the decision has been made.'

'I don't think the Chief was aware of our recommendations when you met him last. But he was indeed being sarcastic and had reasons to be so. Your predecessors had no time to raise and run sources or to keep track of what their junior operatives were doing in the field. They either cribbed about administrative issues or used their posting to expand their financial assets,' Naveen said.

'How many months are you giving me to wind up the bureau?' Jeev asked.

'One month after we approve your logistical and financial requirements.'

'Only a month? But that's too short a period to pull the shutters down on this huge set up. I haven't had the opportunity to meet the majority of the bureau's employees, or visit any of the bordering units, or review any source reports. How can I draw up a realistic schedule for the bureau's closure while sitting in the office? It won't be easy to decide whom to retain here and whom to transfer, or to guide the field operatives on how to disassociate themselves from their sources unless I meet my staff and operatives and find out their operational difficulties. This requires time, maybe a year,' Jeev argued.

'You need not worry on that count,' Naveen assured him. 'We have already worked out the entire drill, drawn up a timetable and identified dispensable assets. By tomorrow you should receive a communication that will guide you on how to go about this exercise. You only have to work out the logistics and supervise the retreat,' he explained.

'Retreat is the right word,' Jeev snapped. 'You couldn't have found a more disgraced general to lead his troops back to their barracks,' he said.

'I don't know why you are taking it so personally. It's an institutional decision that we all must respect,' Naveen said.

'For heaven's sake, stop patronizing me. The least that I expected from you was a hint of what was awaiting me here. I would not have bothered to rent a house or unpack my baggage, which arrived only yesterday. I don't even know whether we should enrol my younger daughter, Adya in school for a few months or make arrangements to put her in a boarding school in Delhi,' Jeev sounded bitter.

'I know this has put you in a tough position, but I thought you would be happy about returning to Delhi. In any case,

Lucknow is not the place for an operative like you,' Naveen tried to end the conversation on a conciliatory note.

Jeev was in no mood to be mollified and hung up after a perfunctory goodbye. He looked at the clock. It was 7.00 a.m. The caretaker of the safehouse came in and served him tea. As Jeev was going through the morning newspaper, the phone rang again. He picked up the receiver and heard the trunk operator announcing that his lightning call to Delhi was being put through.

'Manini, this is Jeev. I just wanted to check how you and the kids were doing,' he said.

'Don't lie. How come you're calling so early in the morning?' she enquired.

'There has been a development. I wanted to let you know about it, and seek your advice,' Jeev said.

'I suspect you are hiding something. I can't recall when you last sought my advice on any matter,' she jibed.

Jeev ignored her barb, telling her instead, 'I'll explain things when you get here. Has field officer Narayan met you?' he enquired.

'Yes. He is coming to pick us up at 8.00 a.m.,' she said.

'I'll be coming to the airport to receive you,' Jeev said.

'But the flight lands at 11.30 a.m. Will it be possible for you to leave your office?'

'There is hardly anything to do here and very soon I am going to be without a job,' he said.

'That will be the day,' she quipped and hung up.

Prateek Awasthy's face fell when Jeevnathan conveyed headquarters' decision to his deputy. He appeared nervous as he dabbed at the sweat that had broken out on his forehead. Jeev enquired if he was feeling all right.

'If you're not up to it, we can have the discussion later,' he said.

'I'm fine, sir,' Awasthy replied, regaining his composure. 'It's just that this news has come as a complete shock to me.'

'But why should an official decision affect you so much?' Jeev asked.

'Sir, apart from the personal problems that it is going to create for me, this is a thoughtless and untimely operational decision.'

'Why do you say that?'

'We are running several key operations and handling numerous assets of critical importance. It will be insane to abandon all of them suddenly when passions are running so high between India and Nepal. Sir, you know that the Nepalese king is adamant on buying anti-aircraft guns from China, which he neither needs to fight the communists nor to maintain law and order. He has also promised several economic concessions to the Chinese and has offered to give them unfettered access to build roads, railways and military institutions. On the other hand, he refuses to extend the Indo-Nepal peace and friendship treaty and ignores our repeated requests to prevent ISI and Islamic extremist groups from using Nepalese soil to infiltrate Kashmiri terrorists, Sikh militants and Northeast insurgents into India. All our efforts to persuade the king to see the long-term benefits of a friendly relationship with India have failed. I hear Delhi is exploring various options to punish him. Sir, we need the ESB now more than ever to cover anti-India activities in Nepal. Neither headquarters nor its sources in Nepal can do this job effectively without being harassed by the Nepalese volunteers for terrorist operations in Jammu and Kashmir,' he claimed.

Jeev's interest was piqued, but he was careful not to show any reaction to the bait.

'Anwar, you will have to excuse me. The High Commissioner must be waiting for me at his residence. I am already running late for the meeting,' Jeev said firmly, not bothering to hide his discomfort at the walk-in's continued presence.

He then ushered Anwar out of his office, locked the room and headed to the lift. Anwar, who followed him down to the parking area in the basement, seemed familiar with the layout of the High Commission's building.

'I also know where Indian insurgents are located in Bangladesh and which agencies are providing them with logistical support,' Anwar bragged as they walked. 'If any one of them is on your hit list, give me his name. I will do the rest on your behalf. You can also count on me whenever you need help in pulling off a violent operation.'

Jeev was horrified by the man's audacious declaration of his reach and the tenor of his claims. He thought Anwar had gone too far in his attempt to ingratiate himself with him, but Jeev knew that he could not shake him off easily. He had to be deftly handled lest he exposed Jeev and the members of his unit. As Jeev got into his car, Anwar reminded him that he would be waiting for his call.

Jeevnathan had no meeting to attend. He had simply wanted to get rid of Anwar. Within fifteen minutes, he was back in his office, running a floppy disk on which was stored data on all the station's assets, past and present, to search for Lateef aka Anwar, but he found no one matching the young man's description. He then called Bijon and asked him about Anwar.

'Sir, he did meet me on a few occasions but provided no intelligence inputs,' Bijon submitted. 'He would generally discuss political developments appearing in the local newspapers. Whenever I suggested that I would pay him handsomely if he provided information on Jamaat-e-Islami's activities, he would flatly refuse. Eventually, he stopped coming to meet me, but then one day, he turned up with the passports of some of his friends and relatives and sought my help in getting their visas stamped on priority. He was doing it to earn some extra money,' he recalled.

'Did he ever mention to you that he wanted to meet me?' Jeev asked.

'Yes, sir, but since I did not see him as a productive source, I dissuaded him,' Bijon replied.

'Did you ask him why you should help him with visa matters when he had nothing to offer in return?' Jeev questioned.

'Yes, sir. He told me he could be useful in many ways, such as setting up appointments with doctors, buying provisions and fish from the wholesale market and verifying the antecedents of persons before I recruited them as sources. I once thought of using him as a courier for a couple of my operations but dropped the idea because his visits became very infrequent. I also noticed that his heart was not in obtaining visas for his clients; even when I rejected his visa requests, he would neither complain nor persist,' Bijon replied.

'What else did you discover about him?' Jeev probed.

'Sir, he is very talkative and has an opinion on everything, be it politics, sports or religion. His financial position is not very sound and he keeps trying his hand at different things to earn a living. He is unmarried, probably a college dropout, and is responsible for supporting his parents and one divorced sister. He comes across as highly ambitious, willing to do anything to make it big in life, but when it comes to taking up the job seriously, he backs out. He actually wants to earn easy money,' Bijon said.

'Do you think he is a thoroughbred Bangladeshi national? I didn't get that impression because he spoke Hindi so well,' Jeev probed.

'Did you meet him, sir?' Bijon was surprised.

'I did. An hour ago,' Jeev confirmed.

'Sir, he claims to be a Mohajir who, like many others, was stranded in Bangladesh after the liberation war of 1971 and is yet to be repatriated to Pakistan. He speaks Bengali fluently, but his mother tongue is Urdu. One of his sisters married a Bangladeshi national but is now divorced and living with their parents,' Bijon said.

Jeev asked him nothing further. Apparently his attaché had a fairly long association with Anwar, given the amount of information he had on the young man. But how much of it was fiction, was difficult to say.

Later that night, as Jeev was preparing for bed, Manini asked if he had another spat with Ashish. 'I noticed that you were unusually quiet at the dining table and ate without making the usual fuss over the vegetables,' she said.

'No, it has nothing to do with Ashish. Actually, a visitor, whom I have never met before, came and blatantly offered to work for me as a source,' Jeev said.

'Shouldn't that excite you? Aren't you always looking for such people, whose loyalty you can subvert through bribery and coercion?' she responded sarcastically.

'I know you don't approve of my job, but it is too late in my life to change. This visitor is an enigma. I can neither lump nor dump him.'

'I'm sure you will find a way to manage him with your sweet talk and tainted money. I wish you were half as sweet to your wife,' Manini said and switched off the bedside lamp.

Jeev took a deep breath to swallow Manini's jibe.

The next day, Jeevnathan wrote to Madhavan, the head of the international terrorism and departmental security section, describing the highlights of his brief encounter with Anwar and the information provided by Bijon. Madhavan's response arrived two weeks later. Expectedly, it was dismissive and casually drafted. Jeev was not surprised. Madhavan had no patience for details, seldom read files and reports, depended heavily on his subordinates, particularly his slimy deputy, and preferred signing on dotted lines. His day at the office would begin and end with his solving crossword puzzles. In between, he would dispose of files as if that was an evil necessity, respond to official calls perfunctorily, spend hours sorting out his personal and property matters and have lunch with his friends. At 5.30 p.m. on the dot, he would leave for the golf club. He enjoyed his drinks, perhaps a little too much. He was a compulsive talker, showering his audience with half-truths, salacious news and wild opinions on operations. He had a point of view on every subject, however ridiculous it might be, but he still managed to appear highly knowledgeable to undiscerning listeners. Despite his indifferent attitude towards work, he not only survived in the Agency but also prospered.

Madhavan wrote that since Anwar was a walk-in, he should have been banished outright. Such sources popped up everywhere and notwithstanding what they claimed or offered, they had to be shunned like pariahs, he stressed. 'I do not have a shred of doubt,' he commented, 'that Anwar is an ISI/NSI agent and is being infiltrated to identify the Agency's officers in Dhaka and find out their areas of interest and activities. I cannot comprehend why you felt the need to refer this case to headquarters when you should have known from your own experience that walk-ins are universally rejected as plants and treated as unreliable material for source work,' he concluded. Jeev knew Madhavan could not have dictated the reply. He guessed that his fair-weather deputy, always defensive and known for his penchant for putting cold water on any new initiative, had drafted it. He nevertheless agreed with Madhavan's view and decided not to contact Anwar.

But Anwar had different plans. Two weeks later, he called. 'I have an important piece of information to share. Let me know where and when we can meet. It's rather urgent,' he said in haste.

Jeev was perplexed as to how Anwar had gotten hold of his private number. It was not even known to most of his colleagues.

'Will 3.00 p.m. in your office suit you?' Anwar asked before Jeev could respond.

'What is it about?' Jeev enquired.

'I can't share that with you over the phone,' Anwar replied.

'Any time before noon tomorrow will be suitable,' Jeev said. He wanted to avoid meeting him for as long as possible.

'The delay of nine hours will not serve your purpose,' Anwar warned him.

Before Jeev could respond, the line dropped and they were disconnected. Jeev heaved a sigh of relief, but it was short-lived.

Anwar called again. 'I need to talk to you, right now,' he persisted.

'I will be leaving in five minutes for a meeting with the High Commissioner and I don't know when I will be free. So please come tomorrow,' Jeev said curtly. He did not want Anwar to think that he was available at his beck and call.

'You will regret the delay,' Anwar claimed. 'I thought you gave greater priority to your real work than to meeting the High Commissioner. Anyway, I will meet you tomorrow at 4.00 p.m.,' he said before hanging up abruptly.

Jeev was amazed by the young man's understanding of his work and felt that unless he had been coached by the local agencies, he could not possibly conduct himself in such a manner.

That night, as Jeev lay in bed, he reflected on Anwar's taunting reminder of his priorities and the nature of his 'real' work. I don't think I should meet a walk-in who looks like a ruffian but talks as if he has years of experience working as a spy, he tried to convince himself. There is definitely something about him that is both sinister and fascinating, Jeev continued with his prognosis. Madhavan, of course, is fiercely opposed to running him as a source, but shouldn't I at least find out what the boy offered to share that couldn't wait for a few hours? He did sound genuine and worried. What if he turns out to be a great discovery? And why squander an opportunity without testing its possibilities? Is it right for me to avoid meeting him out of fear of being won over by a source? That would be cowardly. But I don't think it would be wise to push him too hard in the very first meeting. The ideal strategy will be to keep the discussion exploratory in nature, particularly around his family. At some stage, however, I must pose inconvenient questions, such as why he is volunteering to work for me and whether he has any links with Pakistani and Bangladeshi intelligence agencies. If he confirms them, then I should tell him that I will have nothing to do with a double agent. The worst that can happen is that he will expose my cover, but those who want to find out about such things are already aware of my background. It is quite possible that, like a typical walk-in, he may provide explosive information tomorrow to win my confidence, but I need to take that with a pinch of salt.

As sleep began to weigh Jeev down, he decided to only listen to Anwar and avoid discussing any operational requirements, security matters or political developments. The meeting was going to be difficult; Anwar would surely push hard for a trade-off. Jeev knew he would have to be very careful in accepting or rejecting Anwar's offer to work for the Agency and would have to stop him from fishing for information about the unit and its operations. But perhaps he already knew a lot. 'A battle of wits is on the cards,' Jeev mumbled. He didn't know when he fell asleep.

'What is it that you wanted to inform me about so urgently?' Jeev enquired as Anwar pulled up a chair and sat down unhurriedly. This time, he was soberly dressed, appeared washed and clean and his long hair had been neatly cut.

'A three-member team from Lahore arrived in Dhaka ten days ago and was lodged in an ISI safe house in Mirpur. They left early last morning for Calcutta, along with an escort provided by the NSI. Their plan is to meet a facilitator there, who will house them till it is safe to travel to Jammu and Kashmir to join other terrorists,' Anwar informed Jeev and then passed him a piece of paper. 'This has the names and addresses of three locations in Calcutta where they are likely to stay. During this period, they have been advised to restrict their movements and interactions with locals to the bare minimum and to keep shifting from one place to the other to avoid detection,' he added, without beating about the bush.

'Are they Kashmiris?' Jeev asked.

'Two of them are Kashmiris and the third is a Lashkar-e-Taiba commander who is probably going to coordinate terrorist attacks against your military facilities,' Anwar said.

'Who has made arrangements for their stay in Calcutta?' Jeev enquired.

'NSI. They have no dearth of contacts in Calcutta,' Anwar replied. 'I wish you had met me yesterday. I wanted you to apprehend them as they crossed the border. You can still try and raid the three locations in Calcutta to nab them,' he added.

'How will they travel from Calcutta to Kashmir?' Jeev enquired.

'I am not sure, but if past precedent is any guide, someone will come from either Delhi or the Valley to escort them.'

'Why do you think I would be interested in knowing the plans and activities of Lashkar-e-Taiba and Kashmiri terrorists?' Jeev probed.

'You're kidding. Don't they pose a serious threat to your security and is it not your brief to keep tabs on such activities?' Anwar retorted, leaving Jeev stumped. 'Besides, I know that you will pay me for such critical information. I am told by your sources that you pay very well,' he added.

'So you know that we run sources and pay them well,' Jeev repeated, looking him straight in the eye.

'Precisely.'

'Which sources are you in touch with?' Jeev asked.

'I won't give the names,' Anwar replied, his face a serious mask.

'How much do you think I will pay you for this information?'

'I don't expect anything since this is the first piece of information I have given you. I am in no hurry for money. I can wait. I know that eventually you will pay me a lot,' Anwar said, smiling for the first time.

'How big is your family?' Jeev changed tack to verify how truthful Anwar had been to Bijon in giving the details of his family.

'I would rather not discuss my family matters,' Anwar said.

'Fine, let me first verify that the addresses in Calcutta are genuine,' Jeev said. Then he confronted Anwar with what had been bothering him since their encounter began. 'Can you assure me that you are not working for ISI or NSI and that you have not been sent by them to infiltrate our set-up?' he asked bluntly.

'I do work for them, but I am not here as their agent-on-mission. I work for the ISI as a courier, purely out of financial necessity. As for the NSI, I work for them mainly for reasons of survival. Their goons keep coming to our camps to harass us, accusing us of plotting against the government in Dhaka at the behest of Pakistan,' Anwar explained. 'Have you ever visited these camps?' he asked.

'No.'

'You should come and see the miserable conditions in which we live there—stateless and waiting since 1971 for Islamabad to take us back to our rightful home,' he paused. 'That's the reason why Bangladeshis derisively call us "stranded Pakistanis".'

'I cannot understand why an ISI courier wants to work for me unless he intends to double-cross the Agency,' Jeev argued.

Anwar kept silent, appearing thoughtful. Then he explained. 'I disapprove of the obsession of these agencies to destabilize India. I really like your country and have visited it many times. Illegally, of course. My grandfather came from Aligarh in Uttar Pradesh and I still have many relatives there.'

'It is very difficult for me to trust sources like you who volunteer to work for us,' Jeev pointed out. 'I cannot believe that the ISI and NSI aren't aware that you are sitting with me right now, sharing information about Kashmiri terrorists who were trained by them and are waiting in Calcutta to be launched by their surrogates. How do you expect me to be sure that you will not brief them as soon as you leave this building?' Jeev asked.

'I am not your source nor intend to be one. I just want to help. I guess you have never met someone like me before,' Anwar remarked.

A deafening silence ensued.

'I suggest we avoid meeting each other,' Jeev finally took the bull by its horns.

'That is ultimately your choice. I have been following you for the past year and a half. I was particularly impressed by the way you built your relationships with targets and made them work for you, not as sources but as committed volunteers. Their loyalty to you always amazed me. I thought you were very different, aggressive and willing to take chances without being seen. I marvelled at how you recruited Jamaat's assistant secretary general. He is one man who has been virulently anti-India and a diehard ideologue of the party. No Indian diplomat before you was able to even meet him, but see what you have done to him. He now figures on your rolls as one of your most productive sources,' Anwar said.

Jeev was taken aback by the man's access and maturity, which defied his age and appearance.

'How do you know all this?' Jeev enquired.

'Don't worry about that. Neither the ISI nor NSI even suspect your Jamaat source. Actually, I also work for him, escorting his men to Calcutta and other places in India, for which he pays handsomely,' Anwar said.

'Give me some time to think over your offer. In view of your links with Jamaat and the intelligence services of Pakistan and Bangladesh and the work that you do at their bidding for a living, it may not be easy for me to convince my seniors to enlist you as a source,' Jeev said.

'I think you misunderstood me. As I said, I am not here to become your source. I just want to see you go back to India with your head held high as an outstanding operator. So, when do we meet next?' Anwar asked as he got up to leave.

'I will call you,' Jeev parried.

'You must be careful if you do that—your calls are regularly intercepted, so you should use a crypto device to block surveillance. I don't know whether you have one. Anyway, I will come and see you after two weeks,' Anwar said before leaving.

As he watched him walk out of his office, Jeev regretted not having video recorded his conversation with Anwar. It would have been a priceless record of a classic confrontation between an agent and an operative for the archives of the Agency. Manini would have also enjoyed the sight immensely, seeing her husband miserably fail in fending off the challenge repeatedly thrown at him by a rookie.

For two days, Jeev took no action. He was busy reporting on a series of agitations organized by opposition political parties that had virtually paralysed the city. However, Jeev's disquiet over his last meeting with Anwar remained. He wondered how to make the best use of the walk-in without revealing too much of the Agency's operational priorities but was nowhere near having any clarity. Finally, he forwarded to Madhavan the names of the three terrorists as well as the addresses of the safe houses and requested him to verify whether they were indeed staying at those locations in Calcutta, en route to Jammu and Kashmir. He attributed the information to Anwar despite knowing that Madhavan would trash it and ignore its seriousness. But he had no choice. He could neither verify the information independently nor expect Madhavan to initiate an inquiry unless the source was mentioned.

Two weeks went by, but there was no response from Madhavan. Finally, the day before Anwar was to drop by again, Jeev received a cable from his superior—the addresses were correct, but no persons going by the given names were found to be staying there. Two of the houses in the Topshia Tengra area belonged to reputed persons—a doctor and the owner of a restaurant, respectively—and the third one was a mosque in Nakhoda.

When Jeev told Anwar what he had found out, the latter was dismissive.

'What better hiding places than the houses of reputed people and a mosque?' he pointed out. 'In any case, your officers were much too late in verifying my information. By the time they got around to making their enquiries, the terrorists had already reached Jammu, and they are now waiting for an opportune moment to enter the Valley,' he said.

'How can you say this with such certainty?' Jeev asked.

'I met the courier who had escorted the terrorists to Calcutta. He is employed both by Jamaat and ISI on a contractual basis for escorting their boys to India. He gave me the date and time when the terrorists left Calcutta. All three had stayed in the doctor's house and were looked after by a person called Riaz, a Bangladeshi illegal migrant who runs a plumbing agency,' Anwar said.

Jeev remained silent. 'I don't know whom to trust, you or my officers in Delhi,' he finally said.

'You have to cut short your reaction time to such critical inputs and make your officers move swiftly. Do you think terrorists will wait for you to apprehend them at your convenience and at the time of your choosing?' Anwar mocked him.

'I agree. Let me know when the next batch of terrorists arrive,' Jeev said, hinting that the meeting was over, but Anwar made no move to leave.

'I am not so sure about that. Since you have to depend on others to follow up on leads, there is no point in my taking undue risks to obtain the details about the movement of terrorists,' Anwar countered.

Jeev said nothing.

After a few moments of silence, Anwar took Jeev completely by surprise. 'Will you pay me two thousand taka?' he asked. 'I have to take a friend and his contact out for lunch to obtain information on someone that you would never even dream of,' he said.

'What dream are you talking about?' Jeev asked.

'I can clean up Anup Chetia, Secretary General of the United Liberation Front of Assam, before he turns into a monster and a permanent thorn in the side of your security establishment,' Anwar said coolly.

'What is your interest in Chetia?' Jeev quizzed him.

'I thought you would be more interested in getting rid of him than in my motive. The problem with your Agency is that it allows a wound to fester till it reaches a malignant stage. Why can't you methodically dispose of Kashmiri separatists and Assamese insurgent leaders so as to strangle their movement to death? You should learn something from the ISI,' Anwar remarked contemptuously.

Jeev was amused by Anwar's provocation.

'Is Chetia in Bangladesh?' he enquired.

'Don't tell me you don't know that? Everyone is aware of his frequent visits to Dhaka to procure weapons and seek help in training his volunteers and finding safe sanctuaries for their cadre,' Anwar said.

'Is the ISI also involved in training ULFA volunteers and providing them operational guidance?' Jeev asked.

'What will you do with the information if I say yes or no?' Anwar countered.

Jeev had no ready answer.

'Can you at least share his location?'

'He was sighted last week in a camp in Dhaka, guarded by Bangladesh Army personnel to ensure that he is not harmed by Indian agents and word doesn't get out that an Indian insurgent leader is indeed being harboured by Dhaka, as alleged by Delhi. The camp is in a highly restricted area, but my NSI friend knows a contact in the Army who can arrange a meeting with him. He is the same contact whom I propose to take out for lunch,' Anwar confided.

'What makes you suspect that Chetia is being harboured by the Bangladesh Army?' Jeev probed.

'Bazaar gossip. You only need to have an ear to listen,' Anwar quipped.

Jeev did not pursue the matter further. He opened the drawer of his desk, took out twenty-five hundred taka and gave it to Anwar.

'Twelve hundred will be enough for our meal,' Anwar said and returned five hundred taka. 'I may use the remaining eight hundred taka to buy a few things for my friend's personal use. Can I?' he enquired mischievously.

'That is now your money. What you do with it is not my concern,' Jeev said.

Silence followed for a few seconds. Suddenly, Jeev confronted Anwar. 'Are you carrying any recording device on your person?' he asked.

'No,' Anwar appeared unruffled.

'Will you allow me to frisk you?'

'No problem,' Anwar agreed coolly.

Jeev got up and walked around the table. Anwar stood up obligingly so Jeev could pat him down thoroughly to locate any bugging devices. He found nothing.

'I don't blame you. This is only our second meeting,' Anwar said as Jeev returned to his seat. 'Unlike others, you are at least honest in sharing your apprehensions,' he added.

'What is the ISI set-up in Bangladesh like?' Jeev asked as they both settled down.

'I would rather not discuss that. As I told you before, I am in regular contact with two of their officials, but I won't disclose their names. That would be a breach of faith,' Anwar maintained.

Jeev felt himself being pushed firmly on the back foot. He did not recall ever questioning a source from a position of such weakness.

A month passed, but there was no news from Anwar. Jeev tried to convince himself that the walk-in's absence was good riddance, but in reality, he was keen to meet him. Here was an asset who continuously challenged him with searching questions and tested his ability as an operator. Jeev realized that although Madhavan had labelled Anwar as a double-crosser, the latter could be gainfully employed to cover the insurgent and terrorist activities launched from Bangladeshi soil and expose the role played by the ISI, NSI, Bangladesh Army and the ruling government to disrupt India's security situation. Running Anwar would of course be akin to walking on a tightrope, but it was a gamble worth taking. The problem, however, was Madhavan. Jeev had to find a way to either convince or circumvent him.

Jeev thought of writing to Madhavan about his conversation with Anwar regarding Chetia, but he decided to wait till he knew exactly what had transpired at Anwar's luncheon meeting with his friend. He called Anwar a few times on the numbers the latter had given him, but the calls didn't go through. Rains, pouring down heavily since early that morning, had disrupted communication in several areas. He tried to call him after lunch and again at 5.00 p.m. as the sky began clearing up, but with no luck. Fifteen minutes later, Manini phoned to tell him that the physiotherapist was waiting for him at home. Jeev told her he would be leaving shortly and asked his secretary to help him lock up the safe and almirahs for the day. Though his backache was not very severe, the doctor had advised him to undergo four weeks of therapy to prevent it from becoming worse. As he was putting some debriefing papers in his briefcase to carry home to review, his secretary buzzed him.

'Sir, Anwar wants to meet you,' he said.

'Where is he?' Jeev asked.

'Sir, he just walked in and is sitting with me,' his secretary informed him.

'Send him in,' Jeev said.

'I called you several times to find out what transpired in your meeting with your friend, but no one answered,' Jeev complained as Anwar pulled up a chair and sat down.

'I had to leave for Guwahati suddenly to deliver a message to our Jamaat's Indian counterparts. Since we do not take the designated routes or travel with proper documents, it takes much longer to make the journey. I returned only last night. I wanted to come and see you this morning, but the rains prevented me,' Anwar said.

'What was so important that you had to leave all of a sudden?' Jeev enquired, not sure whether Anwar would share the information. Nonetheless, he gave it a shot.

'They were to be given the details of the bank accounts to which money is to be transferred from the UAE for Tabligh activities in Assam,' Anwar informed him.

'Will you share those account numbers?' Jeev asked. 'That will help our economic intelligence agencies to keep a watch on the inflow of foreign contributions and take counter measures. Without this kind of money Jamaat won't be able to create mischief in Assam and the other north-eastern states, which it has been doing,' he said.

'I don't think the UAE money is being used for any purpose other than organizing Tabligh work. But if you can give me any evidence that foreign funds are being misused by Jamaat to cause unrest in India or stir up hatred among Indian communities, then not only will I provide you with all the information required to freeze their accounts but I will also make Jamaat pay for it,' Anwar assured him.

'Fine, then let me obtain the evidence for you from Delhi,' Jeev felt exasperated. 'Was your friend's contact able to take you to Chetia's camp?' he asked.

'We did go to the camp, but Chetia was not there. He had left for Myanmar, accompanied by two junior Bangladesh Army officers, to receive a consignment of arms and ammunition; he is not expected to return before two to three weeks,' Anwar said.

'If you know where he lives in Dhaka, why don't you tell me his location? I can provide you with a camera to photograph the area, his camp and the officers who are guarding him,' Jeev said.

'I can, but what will you do with the information? Are you going to blow up his camp and its inmates? I doubt if you have a plan or the will to carry it out,' Anwar jibed.

Jeev refused to let himself be provoked.

'I think I can handle the job better. It will also be safer for you not to get directly involved in such mercenary operations,' Anwar advised.

Jeev didn't know whether to slam Anwar for patronizing him or play along for long-term operational gains. He had been trying to procure information on Chetia's whereabouts in Dhaka through his assets ever since he had arrived in Dhaka, but nothing concrete had emerged. For the first time, Jeev had met someone who seemed to know Chetia's whereabouts and was ready to wipe out the insurgent leader on his behalf without making a fuss.

'Let's go out to talk,' Jeev suggested.

Anwar agreed; they left together and walked down to the parking area.

'What do you expect from me to get him eliminated?' Jeev asked, facing Anwar as they stood near Jeev's car.

'I will not charge you a taka more than what we actually incur on the project,' Anwar replied coolly.

'How much will that be?' Jeev asked.

'You have to first make up your mind and give me a firm commitment. You must understand that if you pull out halfway through the operation, not only will you be exposed but my associates will be arrested, tortured and even killed,' Anwar warned.

'That won't happen,' Jeev said.

'Take your time. I am in no hurry. Anup Chetia hasn't come to Bangladesh to leave soon. Besides, I have two important missions to execute for others in the meantime,' Anwar explained.

Jeev was tempted to find out more about the missions and who the 'others' were, but gave up the idea for fear of being snubbed. Anwar, he thought, was right. He needed time to discuss the matter with Madhavan. Known for playing it safe, it was going to be extremely difficult to convince Madhavan that Anwar's information on Chetia was reliable and that it would be safe to entrust the job to him. Since Jeev still suspected Anwar of being a plant, he didn't know how convincing he would sound while arguing in favour of funding Anwar for this purpose. But he had a gut feeling that there was no harm in taking a chance.

'By the way, did you hear anything about an attack on an army unit in Kupwara some ten days ago?' Anwar's question pulled Jeev from his thoughts.

'Why? What is so significant about it? Such incidents are fairly routine in the Valley,' Jeev averred.

'One of the militants who carried out the attack was killed in the encounter; he was on the list that I gave you,' Anwar mentioned. 'Why don't you get it verified?' he suggested.

'I will,' Jeev promised. He then pulled out his wallet and gave Anwar two thousand taka.

'What is this for?' Anwar asked.

'Use it for keeping your friend's contact in good humour,' Jeev responded.

'I would be happier if you could use me more purposefully,' Anwar said as he pocketed the money.

Jeev thanked Anwar and returned to his office. Anwar left the parking area from a rear exit. As Jeev walked into his office, his secretary told him that Manini had called to inform Jeev that the therapist had left after waiting for half an hour.

When Jeev finally reached home, Manini didn't mention the therapist, enquiring instead about his backache. Jeev told her that he had been too busy grappling with a major crisis to notice any pain.

'If that is what gives you relief, then I suggest you pack your bags and stay in the office, settling one goof-up after another,' she quipped.

Jeev chose not to respond. He had his hands currently full with two individuals, Anwar and Manini. Both revelled in cornering him.

Jeevnathan decided not to put down any details regarding 'Operation Chetia' on paper to avoid any possibility of the information being leaked. He called Raj, head of the Asia division and Madhavan's boss, and sought approval to visit Delhi to discuss an extremely sensitive matter. Raj promptly agreed.

Before leaving Dhaka, Jeev rang up Madhavan and informed him of his travel plans. The latter was clearly upset that he had not been kept in the loop by Raj, but he said nothing.

Jeev arrived at headquarters the following afternoon. Since his meeting with Raj was not till 6.00 p.m., Jeev decided to meet the desk officer for Kashmir to find out if the terrorist who had been killed in the Kupwara encounter was indeed the same person whom Anwar had named. The desk officer confirmed Jeev's suspicion.

'Sir, I wish the information on the terrorists' stay in Calcutta had been sent to the desk on time,' he added.

'I sent the names as well as the locations where the terrorists were staying to Madhavan on the very same day that they arrived in Calcutta,' Jeev clarified.

'But from the enquiry report that was forwarded to us by his office, it is evident that the field officers were tasked to verify the details almost a week after the terrorists entered India. The delay gave them plenty of time to escape to Kashmir,' the desk officer said.

'But that's the way Madhavan works,' Jeev reacted, before realizing that he should not have disparaged Madhavan before a junior officer.

'Sir, this source of yours is exceptional. Very rarely do we get timely, actionable intelligence in such detail. We should pay any price to run him and take his inputs seriously,' the desk officer was clearly excited at the prospect.

'I know,' Jeev said.

Later, he raised the issue with Madhavan who brushed it aside, maintaining that 'Siddiqui', the name of the deceased terrorist, was a common one, and it was just a coincidence that Anwar had provided the same name.

'I can understand that, but why did you delay in sharing the information about the terrorists' stay in Calcutta with the desk officer for Kashmir?' Jeev asked.

'On the face it, the information looked very suspicious. You can't act on such details unless a tested source provides it. In this case, your source was a walk-in. I cannot send my officers sniffing around hardened militants based on inputs from a mole who works for the ISI, and risk my men falling into an ISI trap,' Madhavan snapped.

'But hasn't Anwar's information come true? Don't you think you missed a golden opportunity to nab the militants in Calcutta? I cannot understand what trap you are talking about. Your officers are operating in India. How can they fall into an ISI trap on Indian soil while verifying addresses?' Jeev argued.

'If you don't like my decision, you can go and complain against me to Raj,' Madhavan said.

Jeev left the room in disgust. He decided to pay Aveek, who was in charge of high-grade operations, a visit. Aveek enjoyed a formidable reputation of being both an aggressive operator and a brilliant analyst. On his way to Aveek's office, Jeev reflected on his predicament. Madhavan would not accept any information from the walk-in and was likely to simply sit on critical inputs. Although Raj did not think much of his deputy's abilities, he would not displease Madhavan because of the latter's closeness to the Agency's Chief. On the other hand, the desk officer for Kashmir was gung-ho about Anwar's inputs.

Aveek greeted Jeevnathan warmly and enquired about the situation in Dhaka.

'There has been a perceptible increase in Jamaat's presence along the border,' Aveek confided in Jeev while giving his own assessment of the long-term security threats from Bangladesh. 'Given the current situation, I think it would be wise for you to raise sources in madrasas to cover this development closely,' Aveek advised him.

Jeev said he would try and then explained why he was at headquarters. 'Do you think I should take a walk-in's words on Anup Chetia seriously?' he asked in conclusion.

'Of course. How does it matter whether he is a walk-in or a regular source so long as he gives you a lead regarding Chetia's whereabouts?' Aveek said. 'Don't worry, I will talk to both Raj and Madhavan and convince them not to throw away this opportunity. But I have another suggestion. Why don't you carry out this operation on your own? I'll fund the entire project without keeping anyone in the loop,' he assured Jeev.

The idea appealed to Jeev. 'But sir, I cannot put anything about this in writing. How will I communicate my requirements from Dhaka and how will you disburse the amounts?' Jeev enquired.

'That is a minor problem,' Aveek stopped as his secretary came in to inform him that Raj was waiting for Jeevnathan in his room.

'Sir, I will think about what you have said and let you know,' Jeev said before hurrying out of Aveek's office.

He was already five minutes late.

The meeting began with Madhavan trashing Anwar's proposal to take care of Chetia as farfetched. 'I don't understand why you discussed such sensitive issues with a walk-in who has himself admitted that he works for ISI and NSI,' Madhavan shot at Jeev. 'However, I am not rejecting the proposal just yet; I want a detailed blueprint of the plan along with an estimated cost before I take a final decision,' he added.

'We need not paint all walk-ins with the same brush,' Jeev protested mildly. 'Anwar is an exception and has all the ingredients to be our most potent weapon for disrupting the activities of our hostile targets in Bangladesh,' he argued.

'I don't think we should even discuss Anwar,' Madhavan countered, looking at Raj. 'He is definitely being planted in our set-up and will blow us all up instead of Chetia. Sir, Jeev must stop meeting him before he exposes our unit in Dhaka and all our operations,' he insisted.

Raj did not offer his opinion.

'Sir, we have already zeroed in on a few assets who are reliable and discrete. They will execute our plan to deal with Chetia within the next six months,' Madhavan claimed.

'Anwar has told me about your plan and the boys you are in contact with,' Jeev interrupted. 'He believes that you are chasing windmills with a broomstick. These are his words and not mine. He knows your boys and said that he would be willing to bet that they wouldn't be able to provide even one piece of information about Chetia's whereabouts,' he said.

A silence fell over the room.

'Sir, this walk-in is a devil and will devour us,' Madhavan finally said to his boss, completely ignoring Jeev.

Suddenly, Raj's internal phone buzzed.

'I have to attend another meeting, but I want you to wait for me,' Raj said to Jeev after he put the phone down.

Jeev nodded.

Raj left, followed by Madhavan. Forty-five minutes later, Raj returned.

'Is there anything else that you want me to know?' he enquired as he settled down.

'Sir, I would like to take a chance with Anwar. I see no harm in two different, unconnected sources trying to accomplish the same mission,' Jeev argued.

'Madhavan has been telling me about his Chetia plan for a long time. Frankly, I am not sure whether he really has a plan. Let me informally sound out the Chief and others who matter in the government and assess their reaction. I'll get back to you within a week,' Raj assured him.

'Sir, I will not be able to provide the blueprint of the plan that Madhavan has asked for. I am sure Anwar will not give me any such plan nor would it be advisable to put anything on record about this operation,' Jeev pointed out.

'Wait for my word. How is Manini?' Raj asked.

'She is fine, sir.'

'Give her my regards. I wish I could have taken you out for dinner, but I have to leave tonight for Europe,' Raj said.

Jeev thanked him and left. He caught the overnight bus to Jaipur so he could spend some time with Maitri, his eldest daughter. They had a great time together; Maitri regaled him with stories about her more colourful professors and her friends, her chance meeting with the movie star Amitabh Bachhan and their conversation, and of course, she complained about the horrible food at her hostel mess. Before Jeev knew it, it was time for him to leave. Their parting, as usual, was difficult.

The following day, Jeev was back in Dhaka.

The 'word' that Raj had promised never came. It was obvious that Madhavan's views had ultimately prevailed. Aveek called to say that he had spoken to both officers, but it was clear that neither had the heart to proceed with Anwar. He also warned Jeev that Madhavan was going to sabotage the project because he was foolishly stubborn and incapable of planning an intelligence operation of this magnitude. He repeated his offer and asked Jeev to meet him in Hyderabad so they could plan the operation together. Jeev thanked Aveek for doing what he could, but he knew that Anwar wouldn't agree to involve anyone else. Wary of facing Anwar and appearing helpless before him, he told his secretary not to entertain his calls.

'But sir, he is here and waiting to meet you,' his secretary replied.

'Send him in after ten minutes,' Jeev said. He then quickly thought through what he would tell Anwar regarding the Chetia plan and why they should not discuss the matter any further.

Anwar looked happy as he entered the room. 'I returned last week after successfully completing both missions and contacted your secretary for an appointment but was told that you had gone to Delhi,' he said.

'Anwar, I want to be very honest with you,' Jeev came straight to the point. 'Please stop meeting me. It is not in your interest to be seen coming frequently to the High Commission, which is under constant surveillance by the Special Branch watchers. Sooner rather than later, the NSI will take you in for some tough questioning since you are getting nothing from me to keep them happy,' Jeev said. 'I am willing to help you financially since Bijon told me that you don't have a job. I can still run you as a regular source, but for that you will have to submit reports,' he added.

'I told you before that I am not here to be your source,' Anwar interrupted. 'My financial needs are adequately taken care of by my operatives. And if I am working for NSI, why should I worry about surveillance and interrogation? It is obvious your seniors did not approve of the Chetia plan. Don't be disheartened. These things happen. But if you really don't wish to see me, then I won't trouble you anymore. This will probably be our last meeting,' Anwar said and stood up.

'But we can still meet occasionally as friends. I have a parting gift for you,' Jeev said, feeling relieved. He handed Anwar an envelope. It contained three thousand taka.

'Thank you,' Anwar said and put the money in his pocket. 'Can you do me one last favour?' he asked.

'What is it?' Jeev enquired.

'I need a camcorder and four blank VHS cassettes. My friend's daughter is getting married next week. He is keen on videotaping the ceremony. We were thinking of hiring a professional photographer, but it's too expensive,' Anwar said.

'Do you know how to handle it?'

'Yes. I attended a photography course conducted by the NSI,' Anwar disclosed.

'You can collect the camcorder after two days, but don't tell anyone that I gave it to you,' Jeev cautioned.

'I won't,' Anwar assured him and left.

That night, as they went to bed, Jeev told Manini that he had finally been able to end his relationship with the man who had volunteered to work for him.

'It's strange—you seem happy to be losing a source, yet they're the ones who normally provide you with your bread and butter,' she remarked.

Jeev smiled, unnoticed by Manini in the darkness.

Two days later, Anwar came to collect the camcorder and cassettes. Jeev gave him a few tips for taking shots under very bright as well as poor lighting conditions. Then he asked his secretary to send in two cups of tea. As they waited, Jeev took the opportunity to ask Anwar about his parents and why he wasn't married. Anwar, however, was not very forthcoming, saying that since they would no longer be meeting, he saw no point in discussing his work or his personal life. It was evident that he was not happy with the turn of events.

Anwar quietly finished his tea, then pulled out a folded piece of paper from the front pocket of his loosely fitting full-sleeve shirt and handed it to Jeev.

'I didn't want to give this to you earlier and cause problems. But since I don't take anything for free, this is a quid-pro-quo for the camcorder,' he said.

'What is this?' Jeev asked.

'It has information on four individuals who first went to Nepal and then entered Bangladesh using forged Pakistani passports. Three of them are from the North-West Frontier Province of Pakistan, probably Afghan fighters, and the fourth one is from Pak-occupied Kashmir, but he is not a Kashmiri. Their fake Bangladeshi passports in local names and with Indian visas have already been arranged and they are waiting to be escorted to India en route to Jammu and Kashmir. Once they are in Calcutta, they will be issued with either bogus Indian voter identity cards or false documents to establish that they are Kashmiri residents,' Anwar explained.

Jeev read the paper.

'I wish you had brought photocopies of their Pakistani passports so I would at least have had photographs of the terrorists. That would have helped us find out who they are and made it easier for the police to apprehend them during their movement in India,' Jeev remarked.

'Except for what my friend passed on, I have nothing more to offer. However, he told me that these men are tall, fair and heavily built, look ruthless and keep to themselves. Their mission is to train the local Kashmiri militants to plan big offensives against Indian security forces and to discourage them from showing any leniency towards even women and children when conducting raids and assaults,' Anwar reported.

'Why did your friend share this information with you?' Jeev queried.

'I don't know. You need not take it seriously if you doubt its reliability,' Anwar responded.

'Where are they hiding at the moment?' Jeev enquired.

'I didn't see any point in probing further since you were not going to follow up leads in any case,' Anwar taunted.

'Please try to understand. If I have copies of their Pakistani and Bangladeshi passports, we can use them to embarrass the Government of Bangladesh and pressure them to stop sheltering terrorists and providing them safe passages to infiltrate India,' Jeev argued.

Anwar laughed. 'I didn't imagine you to be such a naive operator. You talk like a diplomat. I thought you would use the photographs to whack the terrorists rather than cry before the prime minister. No, I can't give you the photocopies because I don't have them right now nor will I attempt to procure them. The best I can do is inform you when they cross over to India, but if you fail to intercept them, then don't ever ask me for any information on India-bound terrorists,' Anwar threatened mildly.

'Where did they get their Indian visas stamped?' Jeev enquired.

'They are forged.'

'Can you give me the addresses of the places they will stay at en route to Jammu and Kashmir?'

'Let me try.'

'Is it possible for you identify the persons who are harbouring them in Bangladesh?' Jeev persisted.

'No, that would be a breach of my friend's faith in me. Besides, if you are merely going to take up this issue through diplomatic channels, why should I endanger my life and those of my contacts?' Anwar mocked.

Jeev said nothing. Anwar picked up his bag and left.

The following day, Anwar came to give more details on the four militants, but as Jeev was not in the office, he left an envelope with his secretary. In it was a typed note providing the terrorists' real names, the three dates on which they were likely to enter West Bengal, their address during their week-long stay in Calcutta and the Kashmiri names that they were likely to adopt. From Calcutta, they were to travel to Aligarh and then on to Faridabad, where they would wait for an escort from Srinagar to arrive. Jeev found the details to be fairly believable. He therefore wasted no time in cabling the information to Madhavan. The latter wrote back after a week, saying that Jeev should have refrained from contacting the walk-in and that he found Jeev's 'strange obsession' with Anwar to be incomprehensible. He mentioned that he had nonetheless initiated field inquiries to assure Jeev that his protégé's inputs were not being rejected out of personal malice. Jeev replied, advising Madhavan to avoid sarcasm, lest the tele-com operators and juniors in the unit found out about their squabbling.

The findings of Madhavan's field inquiry were along expected lines. The address did exist, but no one going by the names given by Anwar was staying there. The authenticity of their voters' identity cards could not be verified as they were forged. The Nepalese and Bangladeshi immigration had no record of the entry of the named individuals on Pakistani passports. Similarly, the Indian immigration could not confirm the entry of any individuals on the alleged Bangladeshi passports. In his summing up remarks, Madhavan reiterated that Anwar was a crook and had fabricated the entire story at the behest of the ISI or NSI. He wondered how Jeev could be so innocent as to not see through their plan to infiltrate Anwar into his unit at Dhaka. Madhavan's observations had the clear imprint of his deputy, whom Jeev had nearly fired over a case of financial impropriety two years ago but had then let him off with a recordable warning.

Jeev was apprehensive about conveying the outcome of the field enquiry to Anwar. When he finally did, Anwar took it calmly. 'Normally, my information is not wrong, but let me check,' was all that he said.

'Don't go around verifying facts. It is not necessary,' Jeev tried to appease him.

'You don't understand. My integrity is at stake,' Anwar said.

'Anyway, are you done with the camcorder?' Jeev asked.

'I will return it in a week, unless you need it urgently,' Anwar replied.

'No, I don't need it, you can return it later,' Jeev assured him.

Anwar left without having his customary cup of tea. He also refused to accept any payment for providing what he termed as 'spurious information'.

The riddle of Anwar continued to intrigue Jeev. But for being a walk-in, he would have been a prized asset for any Agency. Here was a man who, for inexplicable reasons, was begging Jeev to allow him to assist in his source operations and had no greed for money. Most importantly, he was steadfast in his refusal to reveal the nature of his links with the ISI, NSI and Jamaat, betraying his fierce loyalty to his employers. Unlike a typical walk-in, he never fished for information from Jeev, and in fact was protective towards him. He did not want Jeev to take any undue risks in directly engaging with terrorists and insurgents. There was no doubt that Anwar was unique in many respects, and Jeev didn't want to lose him as an asset. So he decided that he would use him without keeping Madhavan in the loop; he would pay him through subterfuge. Accordingly, he cabled Madhavan with a copy to Raj that he had severed all contacts with the walk-in, in compliance with his wishes.

Within an hour, Raj replied. 'I am sorry for not having written to you on this subject so far. It is good that you have dropped him. No one favoured the course of action that he had suggested.'

That night, after dinner, as they were watching the classic Hindi movie *Aawara*, Jeev shared the day's development with Manini.

'Didn't you tell me that you had decided to keep away from him?' she asked.

'I did, but now I want to use him. I have never met a prospect like him before,' Jeev replied.

'I hope your judgment of the man and using him by proxy don't land you in trouble,' she said.

'He won't let anyone harm me,' Jeev averred.

'You need to remember that you are not liked by most of your colleagues—they may get angry over your duplicity and conspire to create more difficulties for you in your work here. But how is it that you have chosen to discuss a source with me? You have never done so before,' she asked.

'He is unique and very special. I guess I can't help but talk about him,' Jeev smiled.

A week later, Anwar came to Jeev's office to return the camcorder and tapes.

'Have a look at this particular tape in your spare time. You will find the contents interesting,' he said.

'What interest can I possibly have in seeing the video of the wedding of your friend's daughter?' Jeev enquired.

'Please take a look. I am sure you will like what you see and if you have any problem in understanding it, I will come and explain it to you,' Anwar said.

Jeev kept the marked tape in his briefcase. 'Will you do me a small favour?' Jeev asked as he put his briefcase away.

'I won't commit unless I know the nature of your task,' Anwar said.

'A cricket match between Bangladesh and Pakistan is scheduled to take place three days from today. I don't want your team to lose the match. You have to ensure that either Bangladesh wins or the match is abandoned,' Jeev said. Although match-fixing was hardly intelligence work, Jeev was curious to see what Anwar could do, besides helping him in operations.

Anwar laughed for the first time. 'I thought you would give me a tricky intelligence plan to execute. What you are asking me to do is a simple task. But I like this change in you. At least you have started believing that I am capable of doing something,' Anwar remarked.

'How much you will need for this?' Jeev asked.

'Twenty thousand taka will be enough,' Anwar said. He put down his empty teacup. 'Why don't you ask me whether I have been able to gather any details on those militants?' he asked.

'I thought you would have listened to my advice and not checked the facts with your friends,' Jeev replied.

Anwar opened his bag and took out an envelope. 'This has photocopies of the Pakistani passports they used to enter Nepal and Bangladesh,' Anwar said. 'As you can see, they certainly don't look like Kashmiris or Bangladeshis. ISI has a man, Anil Pradhan, at the immigration desk at Kathmandu airport. He ensures that such persons are cleared, for a price, of course. NSI follows the same drill at the Dhaka International Airport, keeping the government in picture.'

'How come the Indian immigration does not have a record of their entry? Are you suggesting that even Indian immigration has an NSI contact?' Jeev asked.

'Why are you so surprised? Yes, NSI has a couple of contacts in your immigration office at Petrapol. One of them is Biplob Ghosh. He stamps the passport with fictitious visa numbers, which are obviously not entered in their records. I have myself seen the passports of those militants. They were stamped and appeared genuine,' Anwar explained.

'Can you give me some evidence that he is stamping passports with fake numbers and receiving money to facilitate the entry of militants in India? I will have him immediately dismissed or even imprisoned,' Jeev was visibly concerned.

'Don't get so worked up. Such things have been happening for years and have now become routine. In any case it will not be proper for me to collect evidence because I am also a beneficiary. And why go after Biplob da?' Anwar asked. 'He is not the only one who is helping us,' he said.

Jeev felt helpless. He wondered whether he should inform headquarters about the goings-on at Petrapol, but who would believe him if he did not have proof to substantiate his allegations?

'You haven't told me how those militants escaped our investigators,' Jeev finally said.

'The address in Calcutta that I gave you was correct. They stayed there for two days, but then moved. The local guide feared that their appearance would give them away and so he housed them at Karbala masjid. They are currently camping at Ahl-e-Hadees masjid,' Anwar explained.

'Have their voters' identity cards been arranged?'

'Not yet. The escort from Srinagar is yet to arrive in Calcutta.'

'What is their travel schedule?'

'There has been a slight change in their programme. They are skipping Aligarh and will now go to Hyderabad first and then to Faridabad before they are escorted to the Valley. You should be ready for some fireworks in the first week of next month,' Anwar said.

Jeev kept taking notes.

'I could have alerted you in advance on the nature of the fireworks, but I won't. You seem to be helpless in intercepting these terrorists in India. Actually that your operational priorities are skewed. You are happier disrupting a cricket match rather than killing your enemies. I really don't know why you are here and what satisfaction you derive from reporting on hartals,' Anwar remarked disdainfully.

Jeev took the barbs coolly. 'You may be right. When should I give you the money for the event, now or later?' he asked.

'Normally I would have insisted on payment in advance, but since you don't trust me, let me do the job first,' Anwar rubbed it in.

'That's not true. You are absolutely reliable. The problem is that I have not been able to make use of your inputs,' Jeev admitted candidly.

Anwar remained silent. After hesitating initially, he accepted five thousand taka.

After Anwar had left, Jeev locked the door of his office and disconnected his phones. He took out the tape from his briefcase and played it on the VCR. He knew that if Anwar had insisted that he should view it, it would have some startling information. But what he saw was a let-down. Parijaat, a young foreign service officer and first secretary in the Indian High Commission, had been filmed at a party. He was drinking heavily and spent most of the evening in a corner of the living room, discussing something animatedly with two men dressed in pathani suits. The guests appeared to be a mix of local businessmen, journalists and diplomats, a few of whom seemed to be very friendly with Parijaat. What Parijaat was discussing with the two men was not clear due to the poor audio quality. However, Jeev did catch him referring to India's strategic priorities in the region, Indo-Bangladesh relations, Kashmir, Indian security forces and the economy. His wife approached him twice, probably suggesting that he mingle with others as well, but he didn't leave his corner. Later, two foreigners and a well-built person also wearing a pathani suit joined them. As dinner was announced and the guests converged around a large oval dining table, a man in light grey suit tapped Parijaat on his shoulder, took him aside to the balcony and spoke to him while eating. Around 11.45 p.m., as guests began leaving, another man, carrying two large packets, accompanied Parijaat and his wife to their car. Parijaat was walking unsteadily and was helped by his wife to somehow stagger along. The hosts were nowhere to be seen. Parijaat appeared to insist that he would drive and refused to part with the car keys, all the while gesticulating at his wife and pushing her repeatedly. With some difficulty, she finally managed to snatch the car keys from him and push him into the rear seat. The man who was holding the packets looked on. Once both were seated in the car, he placed the two packets on the passenger seat in the front and waved as Parijaat's wife drove away.

Jeev took the tape out and switched off the VCR. Then he rang up Anwar, but there was no response. He wanted to know what Anwar had thought was of great interest in the recording and why he had chosen to cover the dinner in such detail. On the face of it, there was nothing wrong in Parijaat attending a party hosted by a Bangladeshi businessman and discussing subjects of mutual interest; it was something that all diplomats routinely did. Nonetheless, Jeev knew that Anwar would not target Parijaat unless he smelled a rat. He would just have to wait for his protégé to turn up in his own time to explain the riddle.

The next thing Jeev did was to call Sandeep at headquarters. Sandeep was an expert at deciphering garbled, unclear audio recordings. Jeev told him about the videotape and requested Sandeep to listen to it and provide him with a transcript of the conversation within a week. He also asked him to ensure that the task remained strictly confidential. Sandeep assured him that he would do the needful.

Three days later, Anwar called Jeev at his residence while he was in the middle of hosting a diplomatic dinner. Jeev guessed what Anwar had called about. The cricket match between Bangladesh and Pakistan had been abandoned a few hours ago, following massive disturbances, the burning of several pavilions and the ransacking of the pitch. What he failed to understand was why the match had been violently interrupted at a time when Bangladesh had been heading for a decisive victory. That was not the plan he had suggested to Anwar. Jeev decided not to take the call as he knew it would be operationally unwise to receive information within hours of the incident on an open line, giving away his complicity.

The following day, Anwar dropped in to Jeev's office, unannounced, and asked Jeev for the promised sum.

'I don't know whether I should pay you,' Jeev responded. 'I specifically told you that the match should be disrupted only if Pakistan was winning. You did just the opposite. You robbed the Bangladeshis of a historic win. That was not our agreement,' he reminded Anwar.

'But I am committed to the boys. I thought you would be happy. If you still have reservations, you need not pay,' Anwar said. He was obviously annoyed. 'Why didn't you come on the line last night? Did you suspect that I would share something with you that might benefit the counter-intelligence unit? You still don't know me,' Anwar taunted.

'I don't doubt your operational wisdom. Actually, I was hosting a party and had to receive a minister and his wife who came in just when you called,' Jeev lied.

'Did you read this morning's newspapers? They are screaming against Jamaat and blaming them for the violence. There are demonstrations on the streets, calling for retribution and the Pakistani team is hiding in the hotel. You can rest assured that when Pakistan plays against you in the final, all of Bangladesh will root for your team. Is that not what you wanted?' Anwar asked.

Jeev could not help but admire the young man's reasoning.

'That's smart thinking. But tell me honestly, did you really organize the disturbances?' Jeev questioned.

Anwar kept quiet as Jeev opened the safe, took out some money, put it in an envelope and handed it to the source.

'It's upsetting to hear you speak like this. I don't know when you will stop distrusting me and for how long I will have to keep proving my sincerity. The harder I try to pass on critical information, the more you think that I am doing it under pressure from the ISI and NSI. It seems I was wrong in believing that you were a different kind of operator and that it would be great fun working together,' Anwar remarked as he pushed back his chair, ready to leave.

'There is a reason for my scepticism. You told me the other day that you work for Jamaat. If that is the case, how could you use their volunteers to disrupt the match unless it had already been decided by their leadership to let loose violence if Pakistan were to lose?' Jeev asked.

'It is better that a few things remain unsaid. You are always one step behind in planning operations. You wanted my team to win. I wanted your team to win with full-throated support from the Bangladeshi crowd. Anyway, I have to go now. Someone may be waiting for me outside,' Anwar said.

'The problem is that you share what you want to but seldom answer my questions,' Jeev remarked.

Anwar made a move to leave.

'You can go, but how do I contact you if I need your assistance?' Jeev asked.

'You don't really require me. But should you need my help, call me on this number,' Anwar said wryly. He scribbled a number on a scrap of paper and left it on Jeev's desk. 'It's a new number. Tell the man who answers the phone that you are Samad and looking for Anwar. If he insists on knowing more, hang up. I will meet you a day after you call, if I am in Dhaka,' Anwar said and stood up.

'Why didn't you ask me whether I viewed the tape?' Jeev asked.

'Because you don't seem to value anything that I do for you. It is better that I leave,' Anwar said.

'I can understand why you are so exasperated with me. Believe me, I have faith in you. It is just that I don't accept anything unless I am fully satisfied. You can blame it on my years of working in the Agency. Please sit down. I need you to identify a few people whom I saw on the tape. But before that, tell me what prompted you to videotape the activities of Parijaat?' Jeev enquired.

Anwar sat down and asked if he could get something to eat. Jeev buzzed his secretary and requested him to arrange for fried fish and pastries.

'He is a black sheep in your mission and sold out to the ISI,' Anwar claimed. 'He is a regular guest at parties organized by officers of the Pakistani High Commission and is particularly close to Sarfaraz, the first secretary, and his counterpart from the Pakistan foreign service. What struck me as odd about Parijaat was that in most of his meetings with Sarfaraz, an ISI officer would be present. I became convinced of his complicity when he told an ISI officer recently that you were from the Agency and gave him a list of officers of your unit. Had I mentioned this to you, you would have asked for evidence, which I didn't have then. My only evidence was the ISI officer, whom I could not present before you. You would also not have given me the camcorder to cover the dubious activities of one of your foreign service officers for fear of courting the displeasure of your High Commissioner,' Anwar said.

'So, you did not need it to videotape a wedding.'

'That's right.'

'Can you watch the tape and name the persons who Parijaat spent the evening talking to?' Jeev requested.

'There is no need for me to see the tape. Of the two men in pathani suits with whom your officer spent most of the evening, one is Sarfaraz and the other, with the trimmed beard, is the head of the ISI. Of the two foreigners, one is a junior CIA officer from the US embassy and is quite friendly with the ISI head. The other is also an intelligence officer, but from the British High Commission. The well-built man in a pathani suit is the defence attaché and the man in the light grey suit is the number two in the Pakistani High Commission. The person who put the packets in Parijaat's car is a junior officer who works under the head of the ISI unit. Both often move together. The host is a Bangladeshi businessman. He owns several companies and visits Pakistan and Saudi Arabia regularly in connection with his business.

He knows a number of important officials and political leaders, particularly the home and information ministers in the present government,' Anwar claimed.

'Let me play the tape. Please point these men out so I can be certain who is who,' Jeev said and switched on the VCR.

As the tape played, Anwar kept identifying those whom he knew.

'But who is that man talking alone to Parijaat in the lawn?'

'Are you sure you don't know him? He is the DGFI Chief.'

'I have never met him.'

'But your deputy Sujal meets him regularly,' Anwar said.

Jeev avoided responding.

After the tape finished, Anwar advised Jeev to instruct his field operatives to keep away from Parijaat and to never discuss their work with him. 'I think they need to be clearly told that he has been softened by the ISI,' he averred.

'Is he on their payroll?' Jeev asked.

'I don't know, but he is generously compensated for his information in the form of gifts. I have no doubt that he is being groomed as an asset for the future,' Anwar warned.

'I have never encountered a source like you before,' Jeev marvelled. 'You admit that you work for the ISI and NSI, you insist that you won't betray them, yet you provide information on their attempts to subvert one of our officers. I don't know how you manage these contradictions and what motivates you to help me in my work,' he wondered.

'My betrayal to my masters is limited to ensuring your physical safety and securing your work. I don't care what the other officers of the Indian High Commission do, whom they meet or how badly they treat their wives. I would never have tailed Parijaat had he not revealed your position and background to the ISI officers,' Anwar reiterated.

Jeev was choked for words. 'There is not a single meeting in which you do not amaze me,' he finally said with some difficulty.

For the first time, the walk-in saw a softer side of Jeevnathan.

Two weeks later, Sandeep returned the tape and the transcripts. The contents were disturbing. Parijaat had shared his views on the whole range of India's strategic priorities and how they were being adversely affected by a minority government in Delhi surviving on manipulation, blackmailing and bribery. He had compromised his diplomatic propriety by speaking about his differences with the Indian High Commissioner on the issue of handling Indo-Bangladesh relations and wondered how bilateral relations could move forward when intelligence officers, posted in the High Commission, were allowed to carry out subversive activities to remove the government in Dhaka and keep Bangladesh on the boil. While discussing Kashmir, he had endorsed the idea of holding a plebiscite in Jammu and Kashmir, arguing that the Kashmiris should have the right to choose their political dispensation, regardless of what Delhi felt. If the political aspirations of the people of Jammu and Kashmir were not addressed in time, he warned, it would lead to unmanageable instability and an endless cycle of violence in the state. He had ridiculed Delhi's paranoia over the prospect of the Valley opting for Pakistan in a plebiscite and opined that inducting thousands of security forces year after year to secure the state only betrayed the Indians' lack of faith in the robustness of their democracy. The intensity of his arguments would increase the more he drank. He was applauded for his 'honest views' by the Pakistani diplomats. While he was being taken to the car, Jeev's ISI counterpart had instructed his deputy to keep the packets in the officer's car and had told Parijaat that they contained dry fruits, a set of six cassettes of Pakistani ghazal singers, a small carpet and a shawl for his wife.

Jeev agonized over this development for days. Parijaat was currently only a First Secretary and did not handle any sensitive section. He was also not involved in the High Commissioner's political and economic decisions. But the fact that he was offering unauthorized views on sensitive issues to his Pakistani counterpart and to the ISI was alarming. In six months he would be promoted and assigned to an important section. If the ISI was trying to recruit him as an asset, he could turn into one of their highly valued espionage agents in later years. Jeev's first impulse was to brief the High Commissioner, an extremely competent and fair man, a stickler for observing the correct manners in personal and professional life and a strict disciplinarian. He was a great support to Jeev and never interfered in his source operations. Knowing his zero tolerance for breach of official secrets, Jeev believed that the High Commissioner would certainly view the matter seriously and take it up promptly with the foreign office and repatriate the officer to Delhi without even waiting for their decision to come through.

But what if the High Commissioner argued that Parijaat's opinions on various subjects were already known and that his conversation that night was nothing more than the musings of a pompous, immature officer who had been carried away by the occasion and booze, Jeev pondered. In any case, there was no video footage showing Parijaat handing over any documents or providing a briefing on classified dispatches to Pakistani diplomats. There was also a possibility, albeit remote, that the High Commissioner might get upset with him for placing a foreign service officer under surveillance without obtaining his prior approval and write to the Foreign Secretary, informing him of Jeev's crude attempt at framing the officer in an espionage case.

Unsure of how best to proceed, Jeev rang up Deepak Gogoi, his predecessor in Dhaka, who was now posted at headquarters, and shared his dilemma.

'Do not write to anyone about this incident,' Deepak advised. 'No one will back you up. Instead, you will be accused of bugging foreign service officers and making baseless allegations out of service rivalry. Just stay out of this mess. If the High Commissioner cannot prevent his officers from being subverted, then you and I cannot help. That officer is his headache,' he said.

'But the High Commissioner has no means of finding out what his officers are doing outside office hours,' Jeev countered. 'How can I turn a blind eye to ISI's attempts to recruit an employee of the High Commission? In due course, he will head an important mission, occupy a critical desk in Delhi or even become the foreign secretary. Imagine the damage that he can cause to national security if his slide into the word of espionage is not halted now. I am afraid it will be a dereliction of duty if I knowingly allow this officer to become an espionage agent,' he argued.

'You are not the nation's sole conscience keeper. Unless you want to be ridiculed and chastised, don't pursue this case. Listen to me, just destroy the tape. You don't have to discuss anything with anyone including the High Commissioner. The better course will be to maintain a safe distance from the officer and drop further investigation,' Deepak counselled.

'Fine, then I will forward the tape to the Deputy Chief and let him decide what to do next,' Jeev said.

'Don't ever make that mistake,' Deepak warned. 'I faced a similar situation years ago. A senior foreign service officer came to my notice for falling into a honey trap laid by a western intelligence agency. Like a fool, I reported the matter to the Chief. He commended me and asked me to probe further. I conducted a detailed inquiry and informed him of my findings. He took it up with the Foreign Secretary who was furious and wanted to know whether the Chief had authorized me to conduct the investigation. The Chief didn't back me up. The Foreign Secretary defended his officer aggressively and accused the Agency of witch-hunting its bright and committed officers. For all my efforts to expose a mole, I earned the displeasure of the government,' he recalled.

'I remember hearing about your case. That's why I thought of seeking your advice on how far I can go in this investigation,' Jeev said. 'I tried to locate the papers related to that incident but couldn't find them.'

'I burnt them before I left Dhaka. You should also destroy the tape and get on with your normal work,' Deepak further advised.

Jeev thanked him and hung up. But he did not trash the tape. He kept it safely in the almirah along with the transcription. Then he called Anwar on the new number and left a message.

As arranged, Anwar met him a day later, at around 11.00 a.m.

'Can you follow Parijaat and videotape his movements, particularly when he meets ISI officers and diplomats of the Pakistani High Commission? I need to have more concrete evidence to clearly bring out his wilful indiscretion in passing classified information on to ISI officers,' Jeev said.

'I can't do it,' Anwar flatly rejected the idea. 'I am neither trained nor supposed to follow diplomats with a video camera in my hands like a watcher from an intelligence agency.'

'My intention is not to get you in any trouble. But I need proof to fix this officer before he turns into a double agent,' Jeev pleaded.

'If you insist, I can convince one of my associates to cover his activities, but you will have to pay him handsomely. My worry is that his lack of training may expose him. However, I can arrange to have photographs of your officer taken with his ISI contacts, if that serves your purpose,' Anwar suggested.

'That won't be enough to secure his immediate repatriation to Delhi. It is legitimate for an officer to mingle with diplomats of other countries at parties and ISI officers are also diplomats in the Pakistani High Commission,' Jeev contended.

'Why don't you bug his office and residence telephones? You must have devices for such a purpose. That will give you clues as to what he is up to,' Anwar suggested.

Jeev simply smiled because he did not have any bugging device in his kitty of outdated surveillance tools.

'I won't press if you don't want to tell me about your devices,' Anwar said, leaving Jeevnathan flustered. 'By the way, are you aware that Parijaat has serious marital issues with his wife? I believe they fight like dogs and frequently get physical with one other,' he mentioned, taking Jeev by surprise.

'Yes, they do fight and at times it becomes ugly. But what has that got to do with his suspicious proximity to the ISI?' Jeev asked.

'Such fault lines in marital relationships are usually exploited by clever operatives to introduce women for softening targets. I am sure you must have done it many times in your career,' Anwar said.

Jeev remained silent.

'You may have noticed in the video that a lady keeps coming up to Parijaat, bending low over him to show off her deep neckline, making polite conversation and then leaving,' he continued. 'Interestingly, she makes her advances only when his wife is not around. What is not in the video is that I saw them entering a room together, but I decided not to follow them for fear of exposure. A couple of days later, I spotted them again at a restaurant,' he added.

'Who is this lady?' Jeev asked.

'She is a Bangladeshi and is often at parties hosted by the Pakistani High Commission. I don't know the nature of her relationship with your officer, but I suspect she is his honeybee,' Anwar explained.

Jeev heard Anwar out but did not ask the walk-in to do anything more for him.

After Anwar left, Jeev rang up Deepak and briefed him on what the walk-in had said.

'If you consider me your friend, please don't waste your time on this incident. Just forget about it,' Deepak urged. 'If you report the matter, the foreign office will ask for conclusive evidence, which you don't have. You cannot produce your friend as your witness either. Why do you have a death wish of being condemned by the Foreign Secretary and abandoned by your department?' he questioned.

'So what you are saying is that I should knowingly let one of our officers be subverted. Tell me honestly, is that the right thing to do?' Jeev countered.

'No, it isn't, but you have a career ahead of you. Don't let it flounder because of a misplaced belief in righteousness. Look at me. Thanks to the government's displeasure over my actions, I am struggling to get my records straight before I can stake my claim for another overseas assignment,' Deepak sounded bitter.

Jeev kept quiet. After several seconds, he broke the silence.

'Fine, I will do as you have suggested,' Jeev said. He had never felt so morally weak.

'That's more pragmatic. Please carry on with your source work and let the Foreign Secretary manage his house. Since you are a dear friend, I don't want you to suffer the way I did,' Deepak remarked.

The line suddenly dropped. Jeev did not try to call his colleague again. He went to the almirah, took out the tape and the transcript sent by Sandeep, put them in an envelope and sealed it. Across it he wrote, 'To be destroyed at the time of departure' and then deposited it in the safe.

In the evening, when Manini was serving tea, he enquired if Parijaat's marital situation had improved.

'It will never improve. The man is a beast,' she said in disgust. 'My blood boils when I hear you talk so politely to him on the phone and at parties. Maybe all men are alike. You should have seen Sonali's face the other day. It had scratches all over it. I told her to write to the Prime Minister but she won't, for the sake of the kids. Sometimes, even kids become a burden,' she said.

'Can you please pass me the cake,' Jeev requested, trying to divert her attention to more pleasant conversation.

For the next two months, there was no sign of Anwar. Jeev got busy with his regular consular and source work, but Parijaat's coziness to the ISI continued to haunt him. Meanwhile, he was summoned by Ashish, his controlling desk officer, to Delhi to remain available while the Chief met with a high-level contact from Bangladesh. After the discussions were over, Jeev flew to Jaipur to see Maitri. As always, they had a great time, eating out and catching up, with Maitri keeping her father entertained with her endless funny stories about her teachers, classes and friends. Jeev returned to Delhi the following morning and as he was taking the evening flight for Calcutta, he decided to call on Raj and brief him on Parijaat's suspect activities. Raj was concerned and suggested that Jeev send him the tape immediately for his viewing. But Deepak vehemently opposed the idea. The last person Jeev met in the office was the desk officer for Kashmir to get an update on the militant situation in the Valley. The officer told him that in three recent cases of terrorist operations, a marked shift had been noticed in the degree of brutality perpetrated by the militants and in their capacity to prolong the confrontation and inflict heavy damages. A few terrorists had also been heard talking in a language that was not spoken in the Valley, clearly indicating the involvement of Arabs or Afghans in the recent spurt in violence, he claimed.

Anwar was right again, Jeev realized. Those men had not been home-grown terrorists. But who would make Madhavan realize the folly of not taking the information given by the walk-in seriously, Jeev wondered. 'Was any foreign terrorist killed in the encounters?'

'Yes, sir, two of them.'

'Do you have their photographs?'

'Not at this moment, but I will have them later this week,' the desk officer said.

'Send me copies of their photographs. I have a point to prove,' Jeev said.

The desk officer didn't understand what Jeev was alluding to but promised, nevertheless, to share the photographs.

Back in Dhaka, Jeevnathan had to control the fallout of an operation that had gone awry, creating panic among three of his field officers. He thought of seeking Anwar's help and even called him, but he was untraceable. However, a week later, Anwar turned up on his own, looking tired.

'I know you called, but I was travelling. I returned only this morning at 4.00 a.m.,' he said.

'That's okay. I was wondering whether you could give me a contact in the counter intelligence unit of the Special Branch,' Jeev enquired.

'No. You know that I don't want to become your talent spotter or a courier,' Anwar reiterated.

'Actually, I am beginning to believe in your information,' Jeev said.

'Do your seniors feel the same way?' Anwar asked. 'I guess you're referring to the information on the Afghan mercenaries. One of them died during a raid and his body was found in a badly mutilated condition. He was carrying a bogus identity card with an assumed name, which is being circulated by your media. His real name is on the list that I gave you,' he paused briefly.

'What about the other militants?'

'I don't know,' Anwar said.

There was a long silence before Jeev spoke. 'You look tired. Why don't you go and rest? We can meet in a day or two to discuss our unfinished issues,' he suggested.

'I'm fine. I was thinking about something else. You may not agree, but the ISI is much smarter than you and I enjoy working with them,' Anwar said. 'First, they brought those terrorists to Dhaka via Nepal on Pakistani passports, bypassing the immigration at both places. Then they sent them to Calcutta on forged Bangladeshi passports where they were provided with a new set of forged documents to travel to Kashmir. And once they were in the Valley, they were given bogus identity cards so that no one could trace their background, should they get killed or caught. Could you ever plan an operation like that inside Pakistan?' he dared.

'Why do you keep throwing in my face that we are spineless and clueless?' Jeev asked.

'It's not that. I want you to outfox them, but you are always reluctant to take me into confidence in order to beat them at their own game,' Anwar pointed out. 'Anyway, would you like to meet that Bangladeshi woman? She is young, attractive and very nice to talk to,' he suggested, changing the track of conversation. 'I can arrange a meeting with her,' he offered.

'Would it be advisable for me to meet an ISI agent?' Jeev probed.

'That depends on you. ISI will be very happy if I give them this offer. They are likely to think that I am providing them with an opening to pull you out of your secure environment. It will then be a test of your operational acumen, whether you get trapped or succeed in winning her over to your side. That may also give you an opportunity to find out the precise nature of her relationship with Parijaat to build your case against the officer,' Anwar said.

Jeev marvelled at Anwar's capacity to keep astonishing him with his professional opinion.

'So you know her, don't you?' Jeev enquired.

'My friend does. She works in the Ministry of Interior as the minister's protocol officer. She is a socialite and quite popular with diplomats. Her liaison with ISI is a part-time occupation.'

'Does the minister know about her proximity to Pakistani High Commission officials and particularly the ISI?' Jeev probed.

'I think so.'

'Tell me the truth. Would you like me to meet her?'

'No.'

'Why are you so protective of me?' Jeev enquired.

'Because I don't want anyone else to work for you,' Anwar replied with a glint of mischief in his eyes.

'Look at the irony of our situation. You are keen to help me but I keep putting you off. Not only have I not done justice to your information but I have also frittered away the opportunity of a lifetime to take on Anup Chetia. I even dumped the investigation against Parijaat for fear of being maligned. It seems I am a waste as an operative,' Jeevnathan poured his heart out. He had never sounded so vulnerable before a source.

There was hushed silence for a few minutes, as Jeev looked out of the large window on his right.

'To tell you the truth I withheld a lot of information because I didn't want to add to your miseries,' Anwar finally said. 'You can now relax since I will be away from Dhaka for at least ten to twelve weeks. I have been asked to accompany nine teams of Jamaat volunteers to Calcutta. From there we plan to go to Nepal and bring in another batch of terrorists for cooling in Dhaka before they are launched in India. If that does not happen, we will go to Siliguri to bring in a few recruits who are to be sent to Pakistan via Dubai for arms training,' he told Jeev.

'Is this an ISI assignment?' Jeev enquired.

'How will it make a difference to your Agency if I deny or confirm it?'

'Will you brief me after you return from your mission?'

'I will, of course, meet you, but don't expect me to share any details,' Anwar said.

'Can you help me in raising sources in the Bangladesh Armed Forces and the NSI?' Jeev asked.

'I can't help you in subverting our army officers. But if I learn of any attempts by the army or NSI to harm your security interests at the behest of ISI or the Chinese, I will certainly assist you in countering them. I firmly believe in a strong Bangladesh, but not as a threat to the security of its neighbours,' Anwar said.

'You know, listening to you talk, I sometimes feel that you are my controlling officer. If you looked older, everyone would take you to be a senior and seasoned officer from one of the government ministries,' Jeev said, smiling.

'I wish I was one of them. That would spare me from my gruelling travel commitments,' Anwar remarked.

'Anwar, you may not want to become my talent spotter, but can you not provide some information on the structure, resources and operational techniques of the ISI and NSI here? That will help me plan my operations better,' Jeev said.

'I don't know why you raise the same topic over and over again. Please appreciate that both agencies pay me regularly and it would be a sin to stab them in their backs. Similarly, I have not mentioned a word about our relationship to them, or to anyone else for that matter. In any case, planning and executing offensive operations is not your forte. It's not that you don't want to, but your seniors are probably averse to taking risks,' Anwar said.

'What would you have done in Chetia's and Parijaat's cases, given the constraints that I suffer?' Jeev asked.

'I wouldn't have involved my seniors. I would have let events speak for themselves. For example, I would have gotten Chetia killed and had photos of Parijaat splashed in the local newspapers showing him in a compromising position with a lady in an ISI safe house. That way, I would have dealt a body blow to ULFA insurgency and cut short the career of a prospective ISI agent. I wouldn't have claimed success for either job, but I would certainly have felt happy in private to have served my country's security interests,' Anwar explained.

Jeev heard him out in amazement and regretted that the same idea had not struck him earlier. He took a deep breath, pulled out three thousand taka from his wallet, put it in an envelope and placed it before Anwar.

'Please don't pay me,' Anwar said. 'You will have difficulty in accounting for the money since I am neither a regular source nor have I provided you with any report.'

'You scare me with your knowledge of how the intelligence business works,' Jeev remarked. 'Don't worry, this is a small amount and I can afford to pay it from my personal savings,' he said.

Anwar took the money and got ready to leave.

'Wait, I want to show you something,' Jeev bent down to open the last drawer of his desk and took out two photographs. 'Have a look at these,' he said and handed them to Anwar.

He looked through them and returned to Jeev. 'This one is Bardar and this one should be Mullah Muttaqi, but where is the third one?' Anwar asked.

'He's missing,' Jeev said.

'He is the most dreaded of all the three and a veteran of the Afghan war against the Russians,' Anwar informed him.

Jeev then showed him two more photographs of militants who had been killed around the same time, but the Agency had not been able to determine their nationality or to which terrorist group they belonged to. Anwar looked at the photographs for a long time.

'I think I have seen these men, but I am not sure. Let me check with my contacts,' he finally said.

After he left, Jeevnathan wrote the names of the deceased terrorists on the backs of the photographs and sent them, along with a note, to the desk officer for Kashmir. Within two days, the officer replied excitedly that a special brief was being sent for the source to cover. Jeev received the brief but shredded it. The desk officer had read it all wrong. Anwar was not a source.

Jeev was pleasantly surprised when Anwar tapped on the door of his office and stepped in, unannounced. He hadn't expected to see him for the next three months, but Jeev was pleased that his contact had resurfaced within only four weeks. He welcomed Anwar with open arms, embarrassing the latter. Though he frequently found himself at the receiving end of Anwar's barbs, Jeev relished their confrontations and respected Anwar's refusal to bend or accommodate. He was one man whom Jeev wanted to introduce to Manini, but he held himself back. He imagined that both would hit it off very well, needling him with relish.

'Good to see you. You're looking very dapper,' Jeev said warmly.

Anwar was dressed in a dark blue blazer and grey trousers.

'Thank you. This suit was a gift from the ISI for helping them execute a difficult mission. I wish I could also do something for you to earn an Indian suit,' Anwar said.

'I hope the mission was not directed against India,' Jeev asked, letting Anwar's subtle dig pass.

'Not in the short term, not as long as you are here. It was to augment ISI's operational presence in one of India's neighbouring countries,' Anwar informed him.

'Is that country Nepal?'

'Please do not interrogate me.'

'How was your trip?' Jeev asked, feeling frustrated at his inability to draw Anwar out despite months of association.

'It didn't go as planned. We were held up in Calcutta longer than expected, so we were able to escort only one batch of volunteers. The travel plans were also changed. Instead of returning to Dhaka, I was asked to go to Guwahati and from there, enter Bangladesh via Siliguri. I had to wait in Guwahati for four days, after which I was told to accompany two Jamaat recruits and six "Indian friends" up to Dhaka. The "friends" were actually ULFA volunteers. We travelled in an army vehicle, accompanied by a guide and two uniformed officers. Yesterday, around four in the morning, Colonel Rehman of Bangladesh Rifles received the volunteers on the outskirts of Dhaka. Three of us went from there straight to Jamaat headquarters,' Anwar said.

'What is their mission in Dhaka?' Jeev asked.

'I don't know because no one spoke a word during the entire journey,' Anwar replied.

'What happened to your associate who went with you to Calcutta?'

'He is yet to return from Nepal.'

'Did you visit any ULFA camp on the way?'

'I am not sure if I can call it a camp. The guide took us to a cluster of seven tents deep in the jungle, where we stayed for the night. One of the tents had arms and ammunition stored in it. I don't know what was in the other tents or how many ULFA volunteers were in the camp, because it was very dark during our short stay,' Anwar recounted.

'Can you pinpoint the location on the map?' Jeev asked.

'No, but I made a note of the area's topographical features, so I can find my way back there. In any case, what will you do with this information unless you want to burn the camp down?' Anwar taunted.

'Can you do it for me?'

'Of course, if the tents have not been removed in the meantime. I am told that the Bangladesh Army keeps shifting the location of ULFA camps to prevent detection,' Anwar said.

'Where are they staying now?'

'I can check and let you know, but only if you promise to use the information to destroy their bases in Bangladesh,' Anwar said.

'Why are so driven to go after ULFA?' Jeev asked.

'I don't approve of Bangladesh training and arming Indian insurgents. You can't use monsters as leverage to serve state policy,' Anwar argued.

A long silence ensued.

'Why have the six ULFA volunteers come here?' Jeev asked.

'They will be trained in assembling and detonating explosives so that they can use them to defend Bangladeshi immigrants during communal violence,' Anwar said.

'Surely this kind of training has been going on for a long time. Can you help me to identify their leaders and the locations where explosives are stored?' Jeev asked persuasively.

'Let me think it over,' Anwar said.

'When will we meet next?' Jeev asked.

'Why, do you have a specific task for me?' Anwar enquired.

'No, but it is always useful to hear about your activities and your comments on my operational weaknesses,' Jeev averred.

'I will not be travelling in the near future,' Anwar said. 'Are you still interested in knowing about these terrorists?' he asked as he returned the photographs he had taken from Jeev the last time they had met.

'Of course. I thought you were still making enquiries about them.'

'They were here for a month and were then sent to India. Both were from Lashkar-e-Taiba and hailed from the north-western province of Pakistan. I didn't ask for their names because, as you know, they are never real,' Anwar said.

After he left, Jeev cabled the gist of his conversation with Anwar to Madhavan and Raj, without suggesting any course of action. He mentioned that he had no option but to meet the walk-in who had dropped in unannounced and had shared the information of his own volition. Neither Madhavan nor Raj responded. Separately, he wrote to the desk officer for Kashmir about the identity of the two terrorists. The desk officer promptly replied, sanctioning two thousand takas as a reward for Anwar.

The next meeting with Anwar began on a relaxed note. Jeev avoided talking about security issues and spoke mostly of the local political situation, which was frequently marred by hartals and violence. Anwar did not seem to have any interest in the political developments and had no particular liking for any political party. But he did confess that he was also partly to be blamed for orchestrating violence to keep the cauldron of hatred between the two mainstream political parties boiling.

'Have you ever felt remorse for killing people who did not hurt you?' Jeev asked.

'You are asking the wrong question. I do a job for which I am paid. Do you feel remorse for subverting Bangladeshis?' Anwar countered. 'I came to see you today on your insistence, but this may be our last meeting,' Anwar said. 'Initially, I felt excited to come to you with information, but now I feel it is all a waste of time.'

Jeevnathan was actually relieved that Anwar was taking the initiative to give a quiet burial to their relationship for he did not have the heart to take the first step to end it. He did enjoy his meetings with the walk-in, but he also knew that they were increasingly becoming an academic exercise and an embarrassment.

'You always wanted to run me as a source and a talent spotter,' Anwar continued. 'I will grant you your wish as a parting gift, although you know how much I am opposed to the idea.'

Jeev waited with bated breath because he knew that anything Anwar offered would be out of the ordinary.

'I can introduce you to an employee of the Pakistani High Commission, a potential source,' Anwar offered.

'What does he do?' Jeev probed.

'He is an assistant in their information section. His name is Rasheed.'

'I don't think he would be of much use. I don't need their press briefings or their daily summary of Bangladeshi newspapers,' Jeev pointed out.

'Don't drop this offer summarily. He is clever, resourceful, enterprising and greedy. He is also willing to take enormous risks. You can exploit these traits to persuade him to obtain information from his colleagues who handle sensitive sections,' Anwar explained.

'What you say makes sense, but such sources usually double-cross and it takes a lot of time before they are really useful since they have to win over others,' Jeev argued.

'My job is over once I introduce him to you. Thereafter, he is your problem. It does involve risk, but I think you should meet him,' Anwar stressed.

'What makes you believe that the ISI won't discover that he is working for an Indian intelligence officer? Are they pushing him to reach me with your help?' Jeev asked.

'I don't know what is wrong with you. What kind of intelligence war do you hope to win if you remain trapped in the constant fear of losing your safety? And please don't give credit to the ISI that it doesn't deserve,' Anwar snapped, clearly annoyed. 'I know Rasheed. We are both Mohajirs and share many things in common. I recently sounded him out on the possibility of his working for Indians to spite the Pathans and Punjabis and he readily agreed. This was about eight months ago. Since then, he has been reminding me about my suggestion, but knowing your cautious attitude and operational limitations, I have been putting him off. He is aware of the danger but is confident that he can outsmart the ISI officers. I must warn you of one thing, however. You will have to pay him a lot,' Anwar said.

'Can you run him on my behalf?' Jeev enquired. He thought it would be advisable to maintain a distance from the source in case Anwar's offer was a set-up, hatched at ISI's behest.

'No. My hands are full. If I commit to being his handler, you will seldom get his reports on time. The most that I can do is to bring you his reports and hand over payments whenever I happen to be in Dhaka. It is you who will have to brief him about your requirements and guide him on how best to expand his network. You will also need to review his work regularly and persuade him to be reasonable in his monetary demands. You may have to work out innovative modus operandi both for exchanging communication and briefing him in person,' Anwar explained.

'Fine, arrange for us to meet,' Jeev said.

'Give me a few days to work it out,' Anwar said casually.

It was fairly late by then and with nothing more to be discussed, Jeev secured the office before leaving. Anwar followed him out. At the western exit gate, Anwar stood for a few minutes, surveyed the area for watchers and when he was confident that no one was around, he walked out. Jeev left through the main exit and was tailed right up to his residence.

~

Jeev was determined not to lose this opportunity to recruit an employee of the Pakistani High Commission as a source. Anwar had offered him a goldmine on a platter and he could not let it go unexploited for fear of running foul of Madhavan. But he would have to adopt a different strategy. He would keep Delhi in the dark about Anwar's role in introducing him to Rasheed, telling them instead that he had met the man by chance in a downtown restaurant and had eventually won his trust.

Anwar took a week to come back to Jeev with his plan for the meeting. It was set up for the coming Friday at 1.00 p.m.

'I will pick up Rasheed from the National Mosque after prayers and drop him off at my friend's house in Mohammadpur,' Anwar began.

'Who is this friend of yours?'

'My associate; he recently returned from Nepal. After I introduce you to Rasheed, I will leave so that both of you can discuss your arrangement, but I will remain in the area to keep an eye out for any suspicious visitors,' Anwar concluded.

'Your plan is too complicated and involves too many people,' Jeev opined. 'I suggest you take him to Bijon's flat and familiarize him with its layout. On the day of the meeting, the three of us will reach there, separately. You and your friend should arrive at least half an hour before me. Let him wait and cool off a bit because sources are generally edgy during their first meeting with operatives,' he explained.

'Okay. We will meet on Friday between noon and 1.00 p.m.,' Anwar said.

Jeev then called Bijon and told him that Anwar would be meeting him shortly to work out the mechanics of an operation.

At 12.40 p.m. on Friday, Jeevnathan knocked on the door of Bijon's flat. As he walked into the living room, Anwar stood up and greeted him formally. Rasheed, who was drinking tea, scrambled to his feet and shook hands with Jeev.

'This is my friend Rasheed,' Anwar introduced them. 'Now you can discuss what you want to. I have to go buy medicines for my ailing sister and will be back in half an hour,' he said and stepped out.

Bijon followed him. It was a command performance by Anwar. He was brief, business-like and wasted no time in allowing the proceedings to begin.

'It is very brave of you to have decided to meet me,' Jeev opened the conversation after they were alone in the room. 'I hope Anwar has briefed you on what I expect from you.'

'Yes.'

'What kind of work do you handle at the mission?' Jeev questioned him.

'I am an assistant in the information section. I can pass on the weekly reports that we prepare, copies of the press briefings of our officers and visitors from Pakistan and propaganda material against your government's policies and activities in Bangladesh. We regularly receive such reports from Islamabad to be fed to the local media,' Rasheed said without blinking an eye.

'How much do you expect to be paid for this work?' Jeev enquired.

'Minimum five thousand taka,' prompt came the response.

'But all that you have promised to deliver is published and openly available material. It has no intelligence value,' Jeev countered.

'That is for you to decide. I thought you would be thrilled to have a source in the Pakistani High Commission,' Rasheed said bluntly.

'That I am. But what else can you do for me?' Jeev asked.

'I can't promise you anything more at this stage. I will have to see whether I can access the offices of the High Commissioner, the defence attaché and the counsellor.'

'What about penetrating the ISI unit?'

'It won't be easy, but I can try. With ISI officers breathing down my neck, I will have to be extremely careful about my movements and how I smuggle out even innocuous papers. For the time being, I will only be able to submit reports that I deal with,' Rasheed clarified.

'When will I receive the first set of your reports?' Jeev asked.

'Right now,' Rasheed said and took out an envelope tucked safely in the inside pocket of his trousers and gave it to Jeev. The latter opened it, removed its contents and cursorily glanced through a press briefing and a weekly round-up of local political developments.

'How do you plan to deliver the reports?' Jeev enquired.

'Anwar has shown me a series of drop boxes that I can use and has explained how and when to approach them. I will fill the drop boxes with reports every week. I will choose which drop box to use, depending on which one I find to be safer at the time of delivery,' Rasheed disclosed.

'That sounds fine. But tell me, why are you taking the risk of working for an Indian intelligence officer?' Jeev asked.

'To earn some extra money. We are poorly paid, even on foreign assignments. The other reason is my hatred for these Punjabi and Pathan officers. They treat us like street dogs and never miss an opportunity to call us refugees, thieves and thugs. I want to teach them a lesson,' Rasheed said bitterly.

'How can I help you in this regard?'

'I will pass on information so you can use it to expose their duplicity in what they profess diplomatically and what they do in secrecy to create disturbances in your country,' Rasheed replied.

'But I can do that only if you provide information on ISI's sources, their terror operations, Pakistan's military assistance to Bangladesh and their political conspiracies aimed at harming our security. Don't you think all this is well beyond your reach to cover?' Jeev questioned.

'Maybe, but I can certainly try,' Rasheed assured him.

'Don't be in a rush to collect classified papers or go around sniffing for information that you are not supposed to know. Move slowly. Since you are under intense surveillance by the ISI, I will not insist on frequent meetings. We should operate through drop boxes for at least a couple of months. But I am open to meting you whenever you have something urgent to discuss. The safest place, however, will be this apartment,' Jeev said.

'What about my payment?'

'I will give you two thousand taka today and gradually increase it to five thousand. This is to prevent you from going on a buying spree, which is bound to raise ISI's antenna. They may question you about any new acquisitions or a dramatic change in your spending habits, which you will find very difficult to explain,' Jeev cautioned.

Rasheed remained silent.

'It will also be wise to take your wife into confidence,' Jeev advised. 'She will be helpful in absorbing the increase in your income and protect you from inquisitive neighbours and colleagues,' he said.

'You should start with twenty-five hundred,' Rasheed demanded.

'Fine,' Jeev agreed. He took out his wallet, counted out the amount and gave it to the source.

With the money paid and Rasheed fully briefed on what he was supposed to do, Jeev sought proof of his employment in the Pakistani High Commission.

'I need it to convince my senior officers that I have indeed met a Pakistani employee and paid him money,' he explained.

'I haven't brought any proof. I first wanted to make sure that Anwar was introducing me to the right person. I will bring it next time,' Rasheed assured him.

Jeev heard a knock on the door and went to open it. Anwar and Bijon were standing outside.

'I have to leave,' said Anwar as they entered, 'but Rasheed, you can stay if you are not finished with your discussion.'

'No, no, I must leave as well; I don't want to stay away from the office for too long,' Rasheed said as he stood up.

After seeing them off, Bijon returned and handed Jeev a piece of paper that had been given to him by Anwar. It had the details of the drop boxes that Anwar had shown to Rasheed. 'These are new and meant only for this operation, lest the source tricks or betrays you', Anwar had scribbled in his hand.

'Anwar's operational acumen is incredible. He would be a dream operative for any intelligence service,' Jeevnathan said as he pocketed the note and left.

Back in the office, Jeevnathan dictated a detailed letter to the desk officer for Pakistan on his meeting with Rasheed and sent a copy of the Pakistani High Commission's diplomatic list, which included Rasheed's name, to establish the genuineness of the contact's credentials. He gave Rasheed the code name 'Termite' to hide his real identity in future correspondences. Jeevnathan also forwarded a copy of Rasheed's particulars to Madhavan as part of the mandatory obligation to keep him in the picture about all sources who were employees in foreign missions.

The desk officer was ecstatic and commended Jeev for his great find. Madhavan, however, expressed his unhappiness over Jeev's decision to run the source himself. It would be better, he pontificated, if a junior officer were to handle Termite, keeping Jeev in the background to control the damage in case the source betrayed the handler.

For the next three months, Rasheed submitted reports regularly and met Jeev once a month for a briefing, but he was unable to steal information from other sensitive sections. The desk officer began to get restive and questioned whether it was worth paying Termite a generous salary for providing routine, open information. Jeev was advised to reduce the source's salary and maintain him on a subsistence allowance. Questions were also raised over Termite's delay in submitting details about his family or proof of his residence in Pakistan. When Jeev apprised Rasheed of headquarters' concerns, the source handed over a photocopy of his identity card. Two weeks later, he began sharing dispatches of the Deputy High Commissioner on local political developments, but the analysts at headquarters found them to be of no significance. Finally, Rasheed managed to steal a few pages from ISI files concerning its financial assistance to Jamaat and anti-India newspapers, which to Jeev's great relief, evoked elated acceptance from headquarters.

~

Jeev's backache returned to trouble him in the humid weather, forcing him to stay at home. Luckily, being Eid al-Fitr, it was a five-day weekend, which gave him ample time to recover. He could also stay indoors and escape the sight of slaughtered animals hanging in butcheries all over the city during the festival. He cancelled all his engagements and except for attending to urgent cables, he spent his time reading and sleeping. On the fourth day, as he joined Manini for lunch, she asked him, 'How is your mystery man doing? I haven't heard you talk about him for a long time.'

Jeev said nothing. He hadn't heard from Anwar since the day he had introduced Rasheed.

'Is he also one of those whom you treat like a king while he is useful and then discard once he outlives his utility? I sometimes wonder why you haven't cast me away from your scheme of things,' she remarked, clearly enjoying ribbing Jeev.

'You are not my source but my source of strength, Manini,' Jeev replied. 'In this case, it is he who has stopped dealing with me as he finds me to be an ineffective operative. In a way I am happy not to meet him because he reminds me of my helplessness and inadequacy as an intelligence officer,' he remarked.

'At least someone has shown you a mirror,' Manini quipped.

'Why do you always have to rub me the wrong way?' Jeev asked.

'Sorry, I was only joking. I think your backache has made you sensitive,' Manini said and changed the topic.

The following day, Anwar called Jeev at his residence and sought a meeting with him in the office that afternoon. He said he wouldn't take up much of his time, but the matter was urgent. Although it was a holiday and his backache was still bothering him, Jeev agreed.

Anwar came at 4.00 p.m. and was shown into Jeev's room.

'I am sorry to pull you out on a holiday, but I need to talk to you about Rasheed,' Anwar began.

'What happened to him?' Jeev asked, clearly apprehensive.

'There is nothing to worry about. He called me several times and insisted that I ask you to give him money to buy a refrigerator. He has checked the price with local dealers. It ranges between fifteen to eighteen thousand taka,' Anwar said.

'What is your advice?' Jeev enquired.

'Ignore his every request. If you do not rein in his greed, he will become a problem.'

'Anything else?'

'This is all I came for. I was supposed to be in Chittagong, but I cut short my visit so I could meet you and ask you to be tough with him when he makes such stupid demands,' Anwar advised him. 'I have to go now, but I'll be back soon,' Anwar said as he stood up.

Later that evening, Anwar called him again. 'Do not call your assets during office hours. When I meet you next, I will explain,' he commanded and disconnected.

Jeev was in a quandary. Every report that was collected from the drop boxes included a note from Rasheed asking for immediate payment of eighteen thousand taka so he could buy a fridge as the summer was at its peak. In his last note, Rasheed had insisted on setting up a date for a meeting and had promised to share reports on ISI's budget proposal for the next financial year. Jeev did not wish to meet him unless he had the money nor did he want to let go of the opportunity to obtain a copy of the proposal. He called Anwar several times to seek his advice but in vain. Finally, he dictated a cable for the desk officer for Pakistan, seeking approval for eighteen thousand taka to buy Rasheed a refrigerator.

The desk officer turned down the request. He was, however, willing to reward Rasheed if the source submitted ISI's budget proposal. In a hurriedly arranged meeting at Bijon's apartment, Jeev informed Rasheed that he would not be able to spare money for the refrigerator because his reports, including the Deputy High Commissioner's dispatches, added nothing new to what was already known through media and published material. Rasheed promptly threatened to walk out of the relationship. But Jeev was undeterred.

'Let's not get involved in brinkmanship. Neither of us will gain anything from walking away,' he said firmly. 'Instead of crying wolf, try to procure secret papers so that I can convince my people to increase your salary substantially. Then you won't have to ask for ad-hoc sanctions,' he advised.

'You are not happy with anything that I submit,' Rasheed grumbled.

'That's not true. We have rewarded you for your good reports,' Jeev pointed out.

'It is impossible to access the offices of the ISI and the defence attaché, but I have managed a breakthrough. I should be getting reports from those sections in a few days, but I don't think even that will please you. I procured classified papers from the office of the Deputy High Commissioner but you find them useless. What more do you want me to do? It was you who told me not to become too active, lest both of us get caught, yet today you are pushing me to do exactly that,' Rasheed argued angrily.

'Calm down. It is not my intention to lose you. But you have to do more. Try to obtain at least the secret and top-secret political dispatches of the High Commissioner, particularly those relating to India,' Jeev urged.

'I can't be choosy. I don't have the luxury of time to read the papers before I pick them up. I have to steal in a hurry. But if you pay me for the refrigerator, I can take the risk. You will also have to give me five thousand taka more for recruiting the High Commissioner's private secretary,' Rasheed said.

'Where is the ISI's budget proposal that you promised to give me?' Jeev asked.

'I haven't brought it. I was not sure if we would meet again after this meeting,' Rasheed said defiantly.

Jeev was tempted to tell Rasheed to stop contacting him, but with the lure of obtaining information on ISI's financial commitments in Bangladesh, he was left with no option but to ignore Anwar's advice under the circumstances.

'Although my seniors are opposed to it, give me a week's time to work out something for your refrigerator. You can check drop box 6 on the tenth day from today,' Jeev said.

'Thank you. You have done your bit. Now, see what I do for you,' Rasheed promised before leaving.

Rasheed, impatient as never before, visited the drop box at five in the morning on the tenth day. He found a slip of paper, an envelope and a typed letter from Jeev, which read:

'The address of a shop is noted on the slip. The envelope has the amount that is to be paid to the High Commissioner's private secretary. Present the slip to the shopkeeper, who has been advised to deliver the fridge along with the sale papers. If anyone questions you regarding the purchase, tell them that the fridge was bought under a two-year EMI scheme.'

That same evening, Rasheed placed five top-secret reports in the designated drop box. One of them related to Islamabad's directive to all its missions abroad on how to counter India's position on Kashmir, Afghanistan and nuclear proliferation. The other provided a calendar of defence exchanges between Dhaka and Islamabad during the next year. The third was a draft budget proposal of the ISI, outlining the purpose for which the money was being sought. Headquarters was pleased with the reports and suggested that Jeev reward the source handsomely. However, when Jeev sought money to buy Rasheed a refrigerator, he received a caustic reply from Madhavan. 'Since when have Agency operatives started doling out home appliances as gifts?' As bad luck would have it, Madhavan was looking after the Pakistan desk in the absence of Prabhat, who was on leave for four days. Jeev ignored the note and kept paying the EMIs.

For two and half months, there was no news from Anwar. Jeevnathan became used to working without the walk-in's shadow looming in the background. His source operations had picked up steam and he was busy with writing a paper on the role played by his unit in changing the political contours of Bangladesh to serve as a guide to young officers on how unfriendly regimes could be changed.

Then one day, Anwar reappeared without warning. Jeev greeted him warmly.

'I have come only to inform you that I will soon be leaving Dhaka and I am not sure when I will return,' Anwar began as soon as he was seated in Jeev's office. 'It could be weeks or months or even a year.'

Characteristically, he mentioned nothing about where he was going or the nature of his assignment.

'Do you have any plans to visit Calcutta during this trip?' Jeev enquired, trying to draw Anwar out.

'I may, but it will be my last stop. I am also not sure when I will get there. But why do you ask?' Anwar asked.

'Two persons in the Bangladesh consulate in Calcutta have come to our notice for indulging in suspicious activities. I am sure you know them. We want to find out whether they are from the NSI or DGFI,' Jeev explained.

'Give me their photographs. I don't have to go to Calcutta for this purpose,' Anwar said.

'I have only their names, but they may not have been posted to the Calcutta consulate under their real names,' Jeev clarified.

'If I find the time, I will certainly try to find out,' Anwar said.

Jeev buzzed his secretary and asked him to organize lunch for both of them. While waiting for their food to arrive, Anwar enquired about Rasheed.

'I hope he has been submitting useful inputs? I haven't been able to meet or talk to him lately, but I trust that everything is going smoothly?'

'Do you know that I eventually paid for the refrigerator?'

'What? Why did you do that?' Anwar reproached him.

'He was insistent and threatened to stop reporting unless I agreed,' Jeev said.

'I warned you about his greed. You made a mistake by letting him smell blood, but don't repeat it. If he demands money over and above his salary, don't give in and if he tries to blackmail you, call his bluff by snapping ties,' Anwar stressed.

'But where and how will I get a replacement for him?'

'I can provide another contact, but I guess you won't need any more sources to run now,' Anwar said.

Jeev did not understand what he meant by 'now' and wondered whether Anwar knew about his imminent departure from Dhaka on the completion of his tenure.

'Last week, Rasheed dropped me a note asking for money to buy a washing machine.'

'He's crazy. What kind of intelligence is he submitting to deserve it?' Anwar enquired.

'He has passed on a few classified papers. But what worries me is that apart from making unreasonable monetary demands, he has become very indiscreet in his movements and meetings. He frequently visits Bijon's house to submit reports rather than filling the drop boxes. Can you advise him to keep a low profile? His reckless habits will certainly expose him one day,' Jeev said.

'Why don't you set an impossible target for him? Let him fail and then you can reduce his salary or dump him,' Anwar proposed.

'I tried. He surprised me by producing the defence attaché's secret reports and the ISI unit's weekly summary of events. He also claims to have won over an employee from the Pakistani High Commissioner's personal staff and expects the contact to start filing reports from next week.'

'Let me speak to him,' Anwar said.

They were briefly interrupted as Jeev's secretary brought in their lunch.

'By the way,' Anwar continued when the secretary had gone, 'I thought it might interest you to know that the number of ULFA volunteers arriving in Bangladesh has increased considerably during the past few months. Besides, more non-Bengali boys are now coming to Bangladesh from various parts of India for training in carrying out terrorist missions.'

'Can you give me some details on these developments?' Jeev asked.

'I have asked my friends to collect more information during my absence. I will then decide whether to share the inputs with you or your officers in Calcutta,' Anwar explained.

'You never told me that you were in touch with our officers in Calcutta,' Jeev said, surprised.

'I know many foreign operatives, but don't worry. You don't belong to that herd. I treat you differently, more as a senior member of my family,' Anwar smiled.

Jeev noticed the play of emotions running across Anwar's face. He quickly changed the topic to help Anwar regain his composure.

'The last time we spoke you told me you would explain why I shouldn't talk to sources during office hours,' he reminded Anwar.

'That's when your office phones are aggressively tapped,' Anwar claimed.

'Are the evenings safe?'

'Relatively, yes. But keep evolving different mechops to communicate with your friends,' Anwar said.

'Where did you learn the term "mechops"?' Jeev was curious as the term, a short form for 'mechanics of operations', was typically used only by intelligence agencies and operatives.

'From the NSI.'

'Do you ever feel that passing such information to an Indian intelligence officer is an act of betrayal of your country's security?'

'Not at all. There is a difference between collecting intelligence to protect one's political, cultural, economic and security interests and hurting neighbouring countries by radicalizing their people in the name of religion and destabilizing them by exporting terrorism, which Pakistan does and which Bangladesh occasionally tries to do,' Anwar explained.

'But aren't you also subverting our security interests by arranging for the arms training of Indian boys in Jamaat camps and escorting ULFA insurgents to and from Assam?' Jeev questioned.

'I do these things for my living. But since I don't like it, I wanted you to intercept the terrorists and eliminate Chetia,' Anwar paused before continuing. 'Rather than me, you and your Agency deserve to be accused of weakening India by inaction,' he added.

Jeev was amazed by his logic. He wondered how Anwar could work for the ISI if he harboured such hostility towards Islamabad and was among those who were waiting to be repatriated to Pakistan. He doubted if he would ever truly understand the enigma that was Anwar.

Finding Jeev lost in his thoughts, Anwar left quietly.

That night, Jeevnathan wanted to recount his conversation with Anwar to Manini but gave up the idea, unsure of whether she would appreciate the essence of this unique relationship.

Jeev did not hear anything from Rasheed for almost a month. What added to his anxiety was the fact that the source neither visited the drop boxes nor showed up at Bijon's apartment. When a journalist-contact informed Jeev that two men from the Pakistani High Commission had made enquiries at the shop from which Rasheed had bought his refrigerator, Jeev became seriously worried. The journalist, however, assured him that the Pakistanis had been satisfied after the salesman showed them the record of purchase in the name of Rasheed and the EMIs paid by him so far. Jeev, however, continued to worry. He sensed that something must have gone horribly wrong because the source had not picked up any of the messages that Jeev had left in the drop boxes. It was likely that he had been caught and was being detained and interrogated, preventing him from accessing the drop boxes. In desperation, Jeev called Anwar several times, but the latter did not answer. He had given up all hopes of seeing him, when Anwar suddenly popped up.

'What a relief to see you!' Jeev exclaimed.

'I realized you were desperate,' Anwar said. 'I returned last night and saw several calls from you listed on my phone. I told you that I would not be in Dhaka for quite some time. I've been busy making arrangements to receive nine boys from Murshidabad in West Bengal and send them to the Jamaat headquarters in Chittagong for arms training.'

'Arms training, for what?' Jeev asked.

'To protect themselves against Hindus. That is what the Jamaat training manual states,' Rasheed replied blandly. 'I could have given you their names, but it is too late now,' he added.

Jeev was speechless for a moment. He suspected that Anwar had an inkling of his impending transfer. He quickly changed the subject.

'Did you get a chance to talk to Rasheed? He has neither been meeting me nor sending reports.'

'He won't meet you. His tenure has been cut short and he has been repatriated to Islamabad,' Anwar informed him.

'How do you know this?' Jeev asked.

'He called me in Chittagong a week ago to explain the circumstances in which he was leaving Dhaka. He was questioned at length by the ISI officers about his alleged links with Indian diplomats, but I don't think he revealed anything. His office and residence were also searched, but they found no incriminating evidence. Yet, he was asked to leave within twenty-four hours on mere suspicion. Rasheed was bitter that he was being kicked around because he was a Mohajir. He said that when he met the High Commissioner to put forth his defence, the latter pleaded his helplessness in rejecting the recommendation of the head of the ISI unit,' Anwar explained.

'Did you ask him where he could have slipped to put the ISI on his trail?' Jeev questioned.

'He believes that the watchers of the Dhaka Special Branch may have spotted him while he was going to Bijon's flat and later alerted the ISI. But I don't think that's what happened. No counter intelligence unit ever shares its surveillance reports with foreign intelligence agencies, however friendly they may be,' Anwar remarked.

Jeev was impressed by Anwar's knowledge of intelligence working.

'But how did you manage to buy him a refrigerator, leaving no trace of your footprint?' Anwar asked.

'I sought help from a local contact. It was his ingenious idea. I simply paid the amount required,' Jeev confided.

'I don't believe you. It must have been your idea. I wish you had come up with such inventive ideas to waylay your seniors so that my inputs on Chetia and the terrorists had been used more profitably,' Anwar remarked.

In hindsight, Jeev realized that Anwar was right. He should never have referred to him as a walk-in.

'It's not too late to do the right thing. I can send your information to my headquarters, attributing it to a source in the Home Ministry, after fabricating the profile with your help,' Jeev suggested.

Anwar did not reply. When the silence became burdensome, Jeev finally spoke.

'May I ask you something that I've been wondering about for a long time? I haven't brought it up because I don't want to risk losing you as a friend.'

'Yes, of course,' Anwar said.

'Did you ever feel bad that I paid you so little for providing so many vital inputs?'

'Sometimes, but not because you paid so little, but because you did not make operational use of the information,' Anwar replied.

'You're right. Perhaps I didn't have the acumen to manage my seniors and the authority to have my way,' Jeev confessed.

'I won't blame you for that,' Anwar said. 'But I do get peeved that you still don't share many things with me. Your tenure ends soon and you will be leaving Dhaka early next month, but you haven't told me about this. I wish you could trust me completely, just one time. Anyway, best of luck to you,' he said.

For a long time both remained silent, Jeev gazing out through the window and Anwar watching his reluctant handler. Jeev's guess had been right. Anwar knew that he would soon be leaving Dhaka. Could Anwar really be defined as a classic walk-in or was he a friendly ghost? Jeev marvelled at how such a young man could carry himself with such maturity.

Anwar finally got up and left.

The evening before his departure from Dhaka, as Jeevnathan was getting ready to go for a farewell dinner hosted by a cabinet minister, the guard informed him that one Anwar wanted to meet him. Jeev told the guard to show the visitor in. This was the first time Anwar had taken the risk of visiting him at his residence, but Jeev was not unduly worried. In any case, he would be leaving for India for good in eighteen hours. He also knew that unless Anwar was confident that there were no watchers, he would not take the risk of walking into the house. He told Manini that he was going down to meet a visitor.

'Why did you call him when you knew that we had to go for a dinner?' Manini asked sharply.

'I didn't call him. He came on his own,' Jeev replied.

'I will take another ten minutes to get ready. Don't forget to ask the driver to keep the gift in the car. And please keep your discussion brief. We can't be late for the dinner,' she said.

As Jeev entered the living room, Anwar stood up and greeted him.

'Sir, I won't take much of your time,' he said.

Jeev was surprised; this was the first time Anwar had addressed him as 'sir'.

'I came only to give you a parting gift. It's a print of Quamrul Hassan's famous painting, *Gorur Snan*. I could not afford to buy the original, but it has been given an original touch by another painter. I am sure you will like it,' he said.

'Thank you, but why gift a painting and not something else that is less expensive?' Jeev enquired, smiling.

'Mr Bijon had once mentioned that you were fond of paintings. Hopefully this will remind you of someone, whom you didn't know how to handle,' he teased.

Jeev opened the gift-wrapping and looked at the painting for a long while.

'It's beautiful. I will cherish it as a priceless treasure,' Jeev barely managed to say, feeling choked with emotion.

Silence descended, with neither of them knowing what to say.

Finally, Anwar decided to speak. 'Sir, did you ever wonder why I was so desperate to help despite your distrusting attitude?' Anwar asked calmly.

'I imagined the ISI and NSI were pushing you hard to befriend me. My assumption was based on the fact that you were never willing to discuss their set-up or operations in Bangladesh,' Jeev answered.

'I do not work for either. I work only for Jamaat. I am also not a Mohajir,' Anwar disclosed.

Jeev was shocked.

'Then who are you?' he asked in disbelief.

'Sir, I am a Bangladeshi citizen, born and brought up in Sylhet. I was sent to study in Deoband in UP for three years. That is where I picked up a little bit of Urdu,' Anwar replied.

'If you are a nationalist and patriot, why were you passing on information about the ISI, NSI and Jamaat activities?' Jeev questioned him.

'As I told you before, I am opposed to any activity on Bangladeshi soil that is directed against its neighbours. I will do anything to protect the security interests of my country, but I will also hamper the government in my own way from pursuing the sort of self-destructive policy that Pakistan is best at practicing.'

'How have you survived in Jamaat with these views?' Jeev asked.

'I know how to stay alive and survive. They can't really dispense with me,' Anwar said.

'How did you collect the information on Anup Chetia and the militants going to Kashmir?'

'From friends and contacts. I would rather not discuss those details,' Anwar said.

'So, was the story spun by you to Bijon about your family background a lie?

'Yes.'

'Is the name "Anwar" also fictitious?'

'That's right. I am Bashir, Bashiruddin Chaudhury. Does the name sound familiar to you?' Anwar asked.

Jeev thought for a while but could not recall knowing anyone by that name.

'You once helped release a source from prison and paid for all his legal expenses, apart from saving his family from starvation,' Anwar said. 'What I found fascinating was that no one, not even your officers, lawyers or the local police, knew anything about who bore the legal expenses, maintained his family, persuaded the prosecution to weaken the case and bribed the judge, leading eventually to his release. I imagined that here was an intelligence officer whom it would be exciting to know and work with,' Bashir said.

'How do you know all this?'

Anwar's ability to surprise Jeev seemed endless.

'Sir, I am that source's brother-in-law. I was repaying your debt to my sister,' Bashir revealed.

'Is Rubaiya your sister?' Jeev asked.

Anwar nodded.

'Why didn't you tell me all this initially? What was the need to build a web of lies? Had I known who you were, I would have trusted you and acted upon your information with greater conviction,' Jeev argued.

'I guess the problem was that I walked into your room and offered straightaway to help in your operations. But there was no other way I could have approached you. Neither of us had time,' Bashir said.

'Nonetheless, I wish you had told me about your relationship with Nayeem,' Jeev said, the regret clear in his voice.

'I didn't want to be your source. My brother-in-law made that fatal mistake and you know how much he suffered for it. My sister, however, always spoke highly of you and wanted me to help you. The best thing about you, she would say, is that you do not make anyone feel obligated to you for helping them and that you render assistance without ever being asked. It was for her sake that I did what I could.'

'Give my regards to her. I hope Nayeem is doing well in his new job,' Jeev said.

'Can you guess my age?' Anwar asked with a glint of mischief in his eyes.

'Between twenty-five and thirty.'

'I am forty-two.'

'But you look so young with your chiselled face and thick, black hair,' Jeev exclaimed, yet again surprised by Anwar.

'And what do you think my educational qualifications are?'

Jeev didn't know what to say.

'I am a civil engineer. I left the job to work for the NSI for a couple of years. But they often resorted to doing things that I did not approve of. Much against their wishes, I later joined Jamaat as a paid employee, mainly to be a saner voice amongst its growing band of violent crusaders. I have not been very successful in my endeavours, but I do get a patient hearing by the leadership,' Anwar claimed.

'Bijon thought that you were a school dropout. I often wondered how you could articulate your thoughts so beautifully in both Urdu and English,' Jeev said.

'Mr Mukherjee is partly right. I dropped out from a local school very early and went to study at a good public school in India,' Anwar explained.

Jeev looked at his watch. He was running late and knew that Manini would be waiting impatiently.

'I must leave for a dinner, but please, you must visit me in Delhi, as my personal guest,' Jeev insisted.

'I always enter India illegally and never go as far as Delhi,' Anwar explained.

'I can arrange a proper visa for you,' Jeev offered.

'No, it's fine. It's better that I bow out with mixed feelings about how we shaped and ended our relationship,' Anwar said. Even in parting, his comments were succinct.

Jeev stood up and walked with Bashir to the entrance foyer, where Manini was waiting.

'This is the mystery man I used to talk about. His name is Bashir,' Jeev announced to his wife.

'But you look quite normal,' she remarked, looking at Bashir. 'I wish I had met you earlier to get some tips on how to tame my husband's pride in his job. Do you know, you're the only source about whom he has ever spoken to me in the last thirty years,' she said.

'Ma'am, Mr Jeevnathan made no exception. I am not his source. I don't know whether I can call myself his friend or tormentor,' Bashir responded politely.

'Let me share a secret with you. I have never seen Jeev so anxious to meet someone and yet agonize over the prospect of meeting him,' Manini confided.

'Ma'am, I didn't know I was so difficult for him,' Bashir remarked.

'I'm sorry, we have to leave,' Jeev finally intervened.

He asked Manini to wait for him in the car while he saw off Bashir.

Outside the main gate, Jeev hugged Bashir warmly and asked him once again to convey his regards to Rubaiya and Nayeem. Overcome with emotion, he was unable to say anything more. Never before had he felt at such a loss for words when cutting ties with a source. But Bashir was different. He maintained his composure, shook Jeev's hand a couple of times and then slowly began walking down the dimly lit street towards the main road. He stopped for a moment at the corner and turned around for one final look at his 'senior family member' before moving on to be lost in the evening's rush hour crowds. Jeevnathan remained standing at the gate, watching Bashir walk away, forever.

Intelligence Services. Only our assets, based in Nepal, can obtain the information we need,' he argued.

'So, what do you want me to do?'

'Sir, we must protest and bring these facts to the Chief's notice. The Nepal desk may not have given a complete and true picture of our potential to perform. The fault actually lies with headquarters and not with us,' Awasthy argued. 'We have been sending reports regularly but they seldom utilize our inputs and routinely blame us for submitting them after long delays. Instead of overhauling the communication system to facilitate the quick transmission of inputs from Lucknow and our bordering units, they have opted to shut down the most productive service bureau of the Agency. Sir, they will rue this decision one day. But by then it will be too late to recover lost ground,' he warned.

Jeevnathan felt that although his deputy had raised valid concerns, his reaction seemed exaggerated.

'Maybe what you are saying has some merit, but it is too late to raise these issues. The Chief has already signed the bureau's death warrant and we now have to abide by it. Since I have only recently taken over in Lucknow, I am not in a position to comment on whether you or Naveen are right. I suggest you start working on a plan of how to pull out from our obligations to long-serving sources and discuss with me the difficulties that field units may face in disengaging from them. In case you think that you have assets who must be retained, please give reasons,' Jeev advised.

Awasthy didn't know what more to say. He got up and quietly left.

Back in his room, he slumped in his chair. He suspected that Jeevnathan had been sent to Lucknow with a specific brief to carry out the ESB's demolition. After twenty-

five years of postings to difficult and faraway places, he had finally managed to come to Lucknow to look after his ageing parents and construct a house, which was now almost complete. Only six months ago, his wife had joined a government school as the principal. His son, a banker, who had moved from Delhi to live with them, had gotten engaged only last week and the wedding was planned for six months later, when the house would be ready. Now all his careful plans seemed to be in danger of falling apart. He was stressed throughout the day, wondering how he would break the news to his family. He cancelled all his source meetings, but shared nothing on the station's imminent closure with his junior colleagues. As he was getting ready to leave the office in the evening, Jeev summoned him.

'I have just received a letter from headquarters. It outlines a detailed plan on how we are to proceed. I didn't expect it to arrive so fast. Apparently Naveen is in a great hurry to shut down the bureau. Have a look at it. You may understand their plan of action better,' Jeev said and handed him the document.

Awasthy took it and left. The more he interacted with Jeev, the more he became convinced that Jeev was a collaborator to headquarters' decision, for he neither betrayed anger nor seemed upset with what Prateek thought was a crazy move.

At home, when he finally broke the news to his family members over dinner, they took it with equanimity. His wife reassured him that they would manage, as they always did. Awasthy could move to wherever the Agency posted him next, while she would stay on in Lucknow to look after the family.

Jeevnathan took a day to reflect over the developments. If the operational performance of the ESB was really as bad as Naveen made it out to be, then it would be best if he wound up the bureau as soon as possible and left, he decided.

The first thing he did the following morning was send out a message to all the officers in charge of the various sub-bureaus, instructing them to come in for a meeting the following Sunday. He wanted to meet them as a group since he would not have the time to meet with them individually and ascertain their difficulties in implementing headquarters' decision. He then left for the airport to receive his wife and daughter, Adya.

Manini's reaction was expectedly acerbic. 'I thought you were a great operator and were sent here to improve the bureau's working. What happened to your claim of being friendly with Rajan and Naveen? Why are they treating you like dirt?' she asked as they were driving back from the airport.

'I don't know,' Jeev said.

'How much time will it take you to wind up the bureau?'

'Not less than three to four months, although Naveen estimates that I may have to stay a few weeks more to ensure that the liaison unit becomes fully functional,' Jeev said.

'Then it is better that we move to the new house and admit Adya in school. You know how easily she can turn the house upside down if she isn't kept busy,' Manini pointed out. Jeev agreed.

On the day of the meeting, there was tension in air as the sub-bureau heads, field operatives and telecommunication officers all filed in to occupy their seats in the conference

room. Everyone was curious about the purpose of the meeting; never before had all the unit heads of the ESB been asked to come to Lucknow for discussions. It was only an hour before the meeting was to commence that the deputy had given them some clarity on the purpose of this summons. He had explained that they would be asked to suggest how to smoothly wind up their unit. The officers were baffled at the timing and suddenness of taking such a major decision. Each one, of course, had his own theory on what could have prompted Jeevnathan to take this ruinous course and wondered whether he was qualified to carry out this task, particularly as he was new to the bureau and was not familiar with the functioning of ESB's different units, the potential of their sources and the problems of the officers and employees. Most of them had never met Jeevnathan before. But based on rumour, they fancied him to be overbearing, overly secretive and unforgiving.

The anxiety was palpable as they waited, trading theories and counter-theories in hushed voices. When Jeevnathan entered, an uneasy silence fell over the room. Everyone stood up involuntarily and then sat down in anticipation of hearing the worst. Jeev strode to the front and briefly surveyed the room but did not see any familiar faces. He then quickly began the meeting. He explained that although it seemed very sudden, headquarters had taken this decision after due consideration, assessing the performance of the bureau's various operations and units. He read out portions from Naveen's letter that commented adversely on the ESB's source work and operations. He, however, avoided naming assets and identifying sub-bureaus that had consistently under-performed.

'You can treat this meeting as a farewell visit to the city,' he said. 'This may also be your last chance to brief me on your administrative and operational problems in implementing the order before you are assigned to your new locations. Please collect your respective plans of withdrawal worked out by headquarters from Mr Awasthy. These will guide you on how to gradually dissolve your relationships with sources and wrap up your operations,' he concluded.

A deafening silence ensued. To break the tension, Jeev invited the officers to ask questions to clarify any doubts they had, or offer suggestions on how the closure could be organized in an orderly manner. After a few seconds, an officer raised his hand hesitantly. Jeev asked him to come forward. He got up slowly, made his way through the room and introduced himself.

'Sir, I am Vidyadhar Banerjee, in charge of the sub-bureau at Patan. I shifted only last week to a proper house after living in a tiny room for a year and half, and I spent all my savings on enrolling my only daughter into a boarding school in Lucknow. I will be financially ruined if I have to move now,' he said in a low voice.

'I understand your difficulties, but I will not address any personal problems in this meeting. This is not the forum for it. Besides, we will all be affected by this closure in some way or the other. I moved to a house two days ago but don't know how long I will stay there. My daughter is with me, but I am not sure whether I should admit her in a school. Headquarters has taken a decision, maybe for the wrong reasons, but we must respect it,' Jeev replied curtly.

Vidhyadhar nodded and switched to raising professional issues.

'Sir, I have been running over a dozen sources for a while now, but not even once has headquarters told me to drop them for providing stale intelligence, or avoid raising such sources in future. So why this sudden realization that we are worthless?' he asked.

Vidyadhar had barely finished speaking when Jeev noticed another hand popping up. The man was sitting in the front row and appeared very nervous. As he got up to speak, he cleared his throat a few times.

'Sir,' he began hoarsely, 'the sudden closure of my sub-bureau will derail the months of effort I put into winning over two important sources. But what worries me more is that now I will have to discard three of my sources whose intelligence inputs have frequently been used and their performance has been appreciated by the Nepal desk,' he pointed out.

Jeev looked thoughtful as he replied. 'If what you are claiming about the quality of your inputs is true, I will certainly bring this to the notice of Mr Naveen. What's your name?'

'Bipin Verma, sir.'

'Would anyone else like to say something?' Jeev enquired, looking around the room. When no one spoke up, he continued. 'I can understand your concerns, but as I mentioned earlier, we have no choice but to follow this directive. In the last few days, I have had occasion to go through the profiles of most of your sources and their inputs. I must say that headquarters has good reason to close this bureau. Barring a few, your assets do not deserve to be on the rolls. They are of low calibre and placed in non-strategic areas. Their inputs are not being used because they cover trivial incidents and bazaar gossip. Similarly, the operations

run by this station are not worth the money and effort spent on them as they are directed against petty targets. However, two field units are exceptions to this. They do produce useful information, but our communication equipment is so archaic that by the time that information reaches headquarters, it is too stale to be even noticed. Given this state of affairs, I don't think we can expect headquarters to review its decision and allow us to continue wasting resources to produce worthless intelligence,' Jeev stopped briefly as his secretary walked up to him to give him a note. He glanced at it before returning it to him. 'Our family and financial problems,' he continued, 'cannot be the reason for perpetuating inefficiency. However, I can try to delay your departures by three months, if that helps you to sort out your personal matters. I will also try to make sure that your arrears and advances are paid on time so you don't have to pay from your pocket for travel. In the meantime, if you can produce wonders, there is a reasonable chance that we may survive,' Jeev stopped as he saw Vidyadhar standing up.

'Sir, what exactly do you mean by "wonders"? We have never been challenged to think big. The targets set for us are usually vague. In most cases, we are simply asked to identify sources on our own and raise them. Since we are not exposed to high-grade operations or given any clear direction, we are unable to look beyond sources of low and limited calibre across the border,' he averred.

'Sir, not only that,' Bipin chimed in, sharing his colleague's feelings, 'the money that we are allowed to spend on our sources is less than one US dollar. It is impossible to lure people placed in higher positions in political parties, the government, defence forces and intelligence with such a small amount.'

Jeev noticed that another officer, standing at the back, wanted to say something. He waved at him to come in front and speak.

'Sir, my name is Alok Raut and I have been in this sector for the last four years. I must have sent over six hundred reports during this period, but not once did I receive any feedback from headquarters. I always presumed I was doing a great job, but now it seems I was mistaken,' he said.

Jeev was pleasantly struck by the candid manner in which young and junior officers were sharing their views.

'Alok, you may still be a good operator. There is no need for self-deprecation. After listening to the three of you, I am hopeful that I can buy at least six months from headquarters to complete the withdrawal. Let's use this period to redeem ourselves and prove headquarters wrong,' Jeev encouraged the officers. He paused to blow his running nose.

'Vidyadhar wanted to know what I meant by wonders,' he continued. 'If you can recruit the king of Nepal or his wife, his prime minister, the chief of the Royal Nepalese Army, presidents and vice-presidents of various political parties, or senior officers in the administration as your assets, then that will be achieving wonders. I will not let money be a constraint in your pursuit of these targets. I know I am asking you to pluck the stars from the sky but trust me, if you pursue such goals with commitment, you will not be disappointed. It is possible that you may not succeed, but I will not judge you on the basis of what you have accomplished but on how much and what kind of effort you put into pursuing the targets. In the meantime, go slow on your current operations and avoid meeting your sources as far as practicable. However, don't drop them like hot potatoes. You never know when you will need them.

At the same time, start identifying high-value targets such as the ones that I mentioned. Do not hesitate to call me or meet me in person whenever you need my advice and keep me posted with the progress in your efforts,' Jeevnathan concluded.

As he looked out at the sea of anxious faces, he wondered whether his words and the fear of the bureau being shut down would shake them out of their inertia, pushing them to do something big, bold and different after years of rusting.

Only time would tell.

The note that his secretary had handed to Jeev earlier contained a message to contact Naveen. Knowing he was probably anxious to hear how the employees had taken headquarters' decision, Jeev booked a call to him but it didn't go through. He then sent Naveen a cable, apprising him of his officers' personal and professional concerns and requesting a three-month extension to wind up the bureau so their transition could be as smooth as possible.

As Jeev was winding up for the day, his secretary informed him that Arvind Rao, head of the communication centre, was waiting to see him. Jeev told him to send him in.

'What can I help you with?' Jeev enquired after Rao was seated before him.

'Sir, I want to explain to you why the communication centre is often unable to transmit information from the various sub-bureaus to headquarters in time.

'Go ahead. I'm listening,' Jeev said.

'Sir, we are short-staffed, the equipment is outdated and no one pays any attention to my pleas to replace it. For lack of operational training, I cannot bring the prime minister or the king of Nepal to you, but I do have ideas on how to cut the transmission delays so that headquarters receives reports

on a real-time basis and you are able to regularly guide the field operatives,' Rao explained.

'And what do I have to do to make you achieve this feat?' Jeev asked.

'Sir, there is plenty of transmission equipment lying unused in the headquarters storage facility. Some of the pieces are brand new and not even taken on charge. Others have been condemned but are still functional. If I can get even four or five pieces of the new or condemned equipment, the results will be spectacular,' Rao promised.

'It will not be correct on my part to request the telecommunication division to spare condemned equipment that is awaiting auction for its disposal. Besides, no one will give you the equipment when the decision has already been made to shut down the ESB, of which your unit is a part,' Jeev opined.

'Sir, my plan may still work,' Rao insisted. 'Most of the time, our division has no idea what the operational branches are doing. It's quite possible that my seniors are not aware of the Chief's decision. Sir, please speak to Mr Gupta—he is in charge of the storage facility. He always has a positive attitude towards problems. I am sure he will listen to you and deliver the necessary equipment,' he said.

Jeev smiled to himself. It seemed his words were beginning to have the desired effect. He pulled out a telephone directory from the drawer of his desk, quickly looked up Gupta's number and placed a call to him. Luckily, the call was put through within fifteen minutes. After exchanging pleasantries, Jeev got down to business.

'I will be sending Arvind Rao to you; our communication centre needs some equipment and I would be grateful if you could send what is needed through Rao.'

'I will do my best, but why don't you also talk to the telecommunication advisor?' Gupta suggested. 'In any case I will have to seek his approval on file before handing over the equipment to Rao.'

Realizing where the conversation was headed—a potential dead end—Jeev decided to be assertive.

'The equipment that Rao is asking for is either condemned and has been waiting to be auctioned for the last four years or is new, but is yet to be taken out from sealed boxes and is lying rotting in the store,' Jeev said tersely. 'I am not going to speak to anyone, including the advisor. I am speaking to you because Rao led me to believe that you encourage junior officers to take the initiative and help them to improve the efficiency of the Agency's communication system. Rao is in any case going to meet you. I will send an undated blank receipt with my signature through him. If you are questioned, put a date that helps you to explain to the advisor that the consignment was delivered long before you joined the Agency. If you still cannot spare the equipment, then call me tomorrow. I will ask someone to break open the store and extract a few pieces,' Jeev said and hung up.

Rao was stunned. This was his first exposure to how far one could test Jeevnathan's patience.

The following morning, Gupta called Jeev. He said that he had spoken to Rao and had directed him to collect the equipment from the store. He was, however, not sure if this arrangement could be kept under wraps for long.

'Don't worry. It's just a matter of a few months. I will have the equipment returned to you before I am transferred out,' Jeev had barely finished assuring him when the trunk operator came on the line to announce that he was

terminating the call as the booked time of three minutes was over.

Four days later, as Jeevnathan and Manini were enjoying their morning cup of tea, a news bulletin on the Doordarshan TV channel, which was playing in the background, caught Jeev's attention. The newsreader announced that Delhi had imposed an economic blockade of Nepal. The news was not a surprise to Jeev. Awasthy had already hinted that some harsh measure against Nepal was imminent. Based on newspaper reports, he had suspected that some form of economic sanction was in the offing. However, he had no interest in agitating over this matter since his mandate was simply to wind up the ESB.

Jeev didn't have to wait long. That evening, a cable from the Nepal desk confirmed the news bulletin, explaining that the blockade had been imposed in retaliation to the king's refusal to both renew the Trade and Transit Treaty and cease acquiring non-defensive weapons from China. It further mentioned that Indian security forces had been deployed along the 1,751-kilometre-long Indo-Nepal border, check-posts had been sealed and non-scheduled entry points were being guarded to block the entry of fuel, medicine, food and construction material into Nepal. The objective, it explained, was to starve Nepal and cripple its economy unless the king agreed to address India's strategic concerns. It ended by requesting daily reports from the ESB's sources on the blockade's effect on the supply situation of essential commodities in Nepal.

The cable signalled what could be a potentially interesting turn of events for the bureau, but it also put

Jeev in a dilemma. He had just directed the officers of the sub-bureaus to stop meeting their sources as far as possible. If he asked them now to task their assets to cover the impact of the blockade, the mixed messages would increase the uncertainty prevailing in the bureau. But these were critical times in Indo-Nepal relations. He could not ignore reporting the situation on the ground simply because the bureau was to be shut down and sources were not supposed to be contacted. Besides, the situation had suddenly opened a window of opportunity for the bureau to test the operational calibre of his field officers. So he sent a cable to all of them, informing them of headquarters' requirements and asked them to use this opportunity to prove their units' worth. He cautioned his officers to use only those sources whom they were confident could provide factual information and could be fully trusted in view of the average Nepalese's intense distrust of India.

The officers jumped at this new glimmer of hope. Sources were contacted and information started flowing in. However, the picture that Jeevnathan pieced together from the intelligence received was a grim one. The enforcement of the blockade was weak. The reserves of essential commodities in Nepal remained at comfortable levels, making Delhi's mandarins cringe. A week passed by but the king remained defiant and there were no signs that he was losing his nerve. On the contrary, he was growing more confident. Every day, he issued bold statements, exhorting his subjects to rally behind him in protecting the honour and sovereignty of the country. Several sources reported that the Nepalese administration was yet to feel the need to enforce the rationing of petroleum products, though transportation appeared to have taken a hit. Shops also continued to do

fairly good business. Police and the Royal Nepalese Army had been deployed in large numbers to ensure that prices of essential commodities did not go out of control and there were no public protests against Kathmandu's mishandling of the situation.

With each passing day, it became increasingly evident that Delhi had blundered in taking this gamble. Meanwhile, the international community began putting pressure on both governments to find a quick solution and appealed to the Indian political leadership not to punish the common man in Nepal for the king's insolence. The Nepalese media stepped up its anti-India campaign, crying foul and urging the king to open up the northern borders to allow supplies from China to flow in. It also warned the neighbouring nations never to trust India, a bully that was taking advantage of its geography to starve Nepal.

In the midst of these developments, Naveen called Jeev.

'We've been receiving your reports, but both the Chief and Rajan want you to also compile a daily summary of the stock position of essential items based on the inputs from your units and send it to headquarters,' he said.

'That's a tall order,' Jeev snapped. 'How can you expect a bureau that is supposed to be saddled with useless sources and is about to be closed for performing badly over the years to provide such information?'

'Please, Jeev, this is not the time for settling scores. I know you are not happy with our decision, but you have to support headquarters in this. The prime minister is livid with his advisors and intelligence mandarin, who he thinks misled him into believing that the reserves of fuel and essential commodities in Nepal would dry up within forty-eight hours of imposing the blockade, forcing the king to

come running to him with folded hands. He is beginning to doubt whether India has the capacity to dictate terms to discipline errant nations in the region. He insists on seeing daily reports on the reserves of fuel and food items in Nepal and monitoring the situation himself,' Naveen said.

'Fine, let me see what I can do. Incidentally, I read a report last night from one of our unpaid, untested sources. I have not sent it to you because his credentials don't inspire confidence. He maintains that the blockade is failing because of smugglers who are operating overtime on both sides of the border. According to him, while the check-posts remain closed, the smugglers are having a field day meeting Nepal's supply needs through unguarded points all along the border,' Jeev said.

'Is the source also a smuggler?' Naveen asked.

'Yes, but a petty one.'

Naveen was quiet for a moment. 'I see. Well, let me know if you hear anything to substantiate his claims. Meanwhile, keep sending us the daily reports.'

The next day was a Sunday. Jeevnathan woke up late and spent the morning reading the papers and going through the reports received from the various units on the stock of fuel and food items in the eastern and southern districts of Nepal. Most reports indicated that stock levels were reasonably comfortable and with the current reserves, the king could hold out for at least two more months. Further, a source claimed that the Chinese had stepped up supplies of fuel and arms to Nepal, although he did not specify the routes, the volume of fuel or the number and description of arms.

Jeev put together a summary of the reports to send to Naveen, and then joined his family for lunch.

'Why have you imposed the economic blockade against Nepal?' Manini asked as Jeev settled into his chair. 'I just heard on the news that because of the blockade, Nepal is running short of fuel, medicine and essential commodities and people are coming out on to the streets, calling for the king to reach an understanding with India so they are not made to suffer.' She paused. 'I'm sure this must be the Agency's handiwork.'

'Why do you always think that the Agency is a devil's workshop?' Jeev retorted.

'Because I have never seen the Agency working on constructive ideas or promoting welfare programmes. You either conspire, destroy or subvert,' she pointed out.

'You talk like a Buddhist monk, oblivious of ground realities and the harsh facts of life. This king has been extremely headstrong and refuses to stop buying arms from China or providing sanctuary to Pakistani militants. Shouldn't our government do something to drill sense into him and force him to stop hurting our security interests?' Jeev asked.

'But Nepal is a sovereign nation and has the right to choose from whom it buys its weapons. I am sure your Chief must have misled the young prime minister into believing that as he is a great leader of a powerful nation, the king of Nepal would dare not disobey him. But instead of demonstrating the prime minister's power, you are making him look like a bully and a fool,' she remarked.

'I can't say much on this subject. My information is as good as yours. But you sound more like one of the king's advisors,' Jeev said with a smile.

Before Manini could respond, the telephone rang. Rajan was on the line.

'The last train to leave for Delhi is at 10.00 p.m. I want you to be here by tomorrow morning. Come meet me at my residence. I can serve you dosas, unless you are keen on having an English breakfast,' he said as soon as Jeev came on the line.

'Sir, is this regarding the closing of the Eastern Service Bureau?' Jeev enquired.

Rajan chose not to answer the question, saying only, 'Keep the visit a secret and avoid mentioning anything about your trip to anyone, including Naveen. If you don't get a train reservation, take the evening flight. I will pay for the tickets. As soon as your departure is confirmed, call my secretary. He will arrange to have you picked up,' he said and disconnected.

Unsure of what to make of the cryptic call, Jeev pondered over what Rajan could want with him. The matter seemed urgent and of a serious nature, but beyond that, he would have to wait and see what it was about. He decided to nonetheless carry a report on the actions that he had taken so far to ensure the smooth closure of the ESB.

Rajan Iyer, Naveen's boss and head of the South Asia Division, was a rarity among intelligence operatives. Slim and of medium height, he looked very ordinary, someone who would not stand out in a crowd. He apparently had a distaste for dressing formally. His shirts in subdued colours literally hung on his shoulders and he wore his weathered sandals as an evil necessity. A man of few words and not gifted with the art of self-marketing, he preferred to remain in the background and shunned talking about himself. However, behind the ordinary looks and self-effacing

manner was a man of enormous courage and decisiveness. His eyes would sparkle at the prospect of operating in unchartered areas and his shoulders would square when it came to taking risks. What set him apart from the crowd was his readiness to back the deserving initiatives of his colleagues and throw unforeseen challenges at an eager operative. He had an uncanny eye for operatives who could deliver and encouraged them to come up with out-of-the-box ideas. A master at disguising operations, it was chilling to hear him suggest violent measures to neutralize targets in his characteristically soft voice.

The breakfast meeting defied all Jeevnathan's guesses.

'I have a job for you,' Rajan said. 'You may have been following the news on the economic blockade. The prime minister is furious with us for not correctly projecting the extent of Kathmandu's resilience. Although we are not directly concerned with the physical enforcement of the blockade, we cannot say this to him and throw up our hands in despair. We have to do something to make the sanctions work. I told the Chief that it is smugglers who are outmanoeuvring us and unless they are deactivated, the blockade will never be enforced fully.'

Jeev suspected that Naveen had probably shared the information provided by his unreliable source on the smugglers' role in sending supplies to Nepal.

'I believe one Raghupati is controlling most of the smuggling activities along the UP-Nepal border,' Rajan continued. 'He is the most powerful mafia leader in your area and is feared by officials and sought after by politicians. He

has been charged in numerous cases of murder but has never been convicted due to lack of evidence. My information is that he is being paid by the Nepalese administration and businessmen to breach the blockade, which he is doing very effectively in connivance with his criminal contacts, unscrupulous politicians, police, immigration and customs officials on both sides of the border.'

'Sir.'

'I want you to meet Raghupati and find out if he would be willing to help us in securing the blockade,' Rajan said.

Jeev looked at Rajan, stunned. 'Sir, you would like me to meet a mafia don and ask for his help in a matter of national interest?' he finally asked.

'Yes,' Rajan's eyes were twinkling.

Jeev fell silent. He thought it was an audacious idea and wondered why a smuggler would give up smuggling to help the Indian prime minister settle his political scores with the king of Nepal.

'Sir, given Raghupati's criminal records, will it be safer for me to meet such a person?' Jeev asked.

'I leave it to you to figure this out,' Rajan replied.

'How much can I offer him if he insists on compensation for his losses?' Jeev enquired.

'Let him quote his price. I don't think money will be an issue. However, since we are running short of time, you will have to hurry up.'

'How much do we know about him, sir?'

'I am told he is inaccessible to strangers and first-time visitors. He is guarded heavily and moves around with an armed escort equipped mostly with unlicensed AK-47 rifles,' Rajan briefed him. 'I recall vaguely that one of your field

operatives once sought his help in settling a dispute over his family property. Raghupati had the matter settled in the officer's favour. Later, his cousins, who were dispossessed of the property, sent an anonymous letter to headquarters, complaining about the officer's nexus with criminals. Your predecessor Rajeev conducted an inquiry and punished him with a recordable warning, which would have been noted in his file. I don't recall the officer's name. I also don't know if he is still working in the ESB. I suggest you discretely check with Rajeev who the officer was and where he is currently posted. If it is necessary, I can have him sent to Lucknow on temporary duty. He should be able to help in setting up your meeting with Raghupati.'

Jeev promised to do his best. Finally, Rajan handed Jeev an envelope. It had an air ticket for his return flight to Lucknow and ten thousand rupees to cover expenses for buying gifts for the don and his wife.

Tracking down Raghupati turned out to be quite an exercise. Jeev began his quest by contacting Rajeev. Although he remembered the incident, Rajeev couldn't remember the name of the officer. When Jeev asked him if it would be possible to review the file on the enquiry, Rajeev told him that it should be available in the Lucknow office. Jeev searched for the file but could not readily lay his hands on it. In any case, he did not have the luxury of time, so he tried a different avenue. He asked his deputy Awasthy if he knew of any officer who had been reprimanded for using the services of a criminal to settle his property matters. The deputy drew a blank but offered to check with the accountant, who was the longest serving employee at the station. The accountant

also had no idea. Jeev next spoke to other officers and staff members in the Lucknow office, but no one had heard of the incident. The breakthrough finally came from an unforeseen quarter. A junior field officer, who had earlier been posted in Lucknow, happened to visit the city on leave and dropped into the office to find out the status of his pending payments. During his conversation with the accountant, the latter enquired if he knew of an officer who had been reprimanded for hobnobbing with a criminal, some three years ago. He identified the officer as Bipin Verma, currently in charge of the Gorakhpur unit, and the criminal as Raghupati. The accountant immediately took him to Jeev so he could tell him all he knew. The officer recalled that Mr Rajeev had not liked Bipin for his argumentative nature and had punished him out of malice by acting on an anonymous complaint filed by Verma's cousin.

For Jeev, the information provided by the officer was a crucial lead.

An hour later, Jeev went to the communication centre and asked Rao to connect him to Bipin via the radio–telephone. After struggling for forty minutes, Rao finally succeeded in getting through to him.

'I am told you are in contact with Raghupati,' Jeev said hurriedly lest the line got disconnected.

There was a pause before Bipin replied cautiously, 'Sir, I used to meet him regularly, but that was years ago. I am no longer in contact with him.'

'I have to meet him urgently. Try to find out if he is in town and whether he will agree to have a friendly conversation in his house, preferably within twenty-four hours,' Jeev said.

There was a long silence on the other end.

'Sir, I don't know whether you are aware that I was given a recordable warning by Mr Rajeev for meeting Raghupati. Because of this, I was not considered for a promotion last year. If I meet him again, headquarters may treat me as a serial offender and punish me severely,' Bipin finally said.

'This time it is headquarters' desire that you meet him. If things work out according to the plan, you may even get promoted this year,' Jeev reassured him.

'Sir, what should I tell him if he insists on knowing the purpose of your visit?'

'Tell him that you are not privy to it and that the purpose will be disclosed when I meet him in person. Also let him know that I would like to speak with him in private since the matter is very sensitive,' Jeev explained.

'Yes, sir.'

'I will wait for an early response,' Jeev said and disconnected.

At six the next morning, Rao hurried to Jeev's residence. He read out a message that he had received an hour ago from Bipin. The meeting had been fixed at Raghupati Tripathy's house in Gorakhpur for 8.00 p.m. on the following day.

Jeevnathan's journey to Gorakhpur was harrowing. The road was bumpy, rutted and non-existent in many places. There were several diversions, all of which were narrow, muddy and littered with stones. The bad roads often reduced traffic to a crawl. It took him nearly ten hours to cover a distance of only 140 kilometres. By the time he reached Bipin's house, it was 7.30 p.m. Although he was exhausted, Jeev politely declined even the cup of tea that Bipin offered, suggesting instead that they could have

dinner at Bipin's house later that night, after they met Raghupati; there was a lot riding on the meeting and Jeev didn't want to jeopardize it by keeping the don waiting. Bipin quickly informed the caretaker of the government guest house that the visitor would check-in late and asked his wife to keep dinner ready.

The drive to Raghupati's house was a tense one. Jeev remained quiet for most of it, thinking about how to approach the don and convince him to cooperate. As they neared the house, Jeev finally enquired if Bipin had had any problem in setting up the meeting at such short notice.

'Sir, initially, he refused point blank, but when I told him that it was the deputy chief of the Agency who wanted to meet him, he agreed to at least listen to what I had to say.'

'Did he ask you about the purpose of my visit?'

'Yes, sir, but I pleaded ignorance. He also wanted to know whether you would be accompanied by armed guards and whether the local police and the administration had been informed about your visit. I told him that no one knew about the trip. But he was still reluctant. It took me hours to persuade him to agree. I think what finally worked was that I told him your name was Amulya Tripathi,' Bipin added. 'He seemed pleased at the prospect of meeting another Tripathy, especially one who held such an important position in the government. Sir, he is a staunch casteist and wields considerable influence over Brahmins in the area.'

Jeevnathan merely nodded.

'But sir, as I was leaving he said that during the entire duration of your meeting, his men would keep a watch on my wife and son and if I tried to play any mischief, he would take them as his hostages,' Bipin said, his voice quivering.

'Don't worry,' Jeev reassured him before lapsing into silence again.

His mind was swirling with thoughts about his imminent encounter and how it would go. This was the first time he was meeting an Indian notorious for his dangerous criminal antecedents, and he was going unarmed and without taking his wife or the local police into confidence. Was he on a fool's errand?

The car stopped, jerking him out of his reverie. They had arrived. Bipin got out of the car and approached the tall iron gates of a well-lit two-storeyed house. He went up to the sentry and spoke to him. Jeev followed. Five minutes later, a well-built man holding a rifle in his left hand came out of the house, walked up to gate and instructed both of them to follow him. The car was to remain outside the gates, he said. Jeevnathan complied dutifully and even offered to be frisked. Their escort said that it was not necessary and led them inside the house, seating them in a large room at the end of a long veranda. Some effort seemed to have been made to spruce up the room in a hurry. The windows and doors had new curtains, the manufacturer's markings printed along the edges. The centre table and four side tables were covered with printed linen spreads. Though the floor had been swept clean, the marks left by heavy objects being dragged across it were clearly visible, and bits of straw were swirling through the room, thanks to the ceiling fans operating at full speed. The lighting was just about adequate. Four bulbs had been temporarily hung up, their wires trailing down the walls. The room had three doors, each kept open, probably to ensure that reinforcements could rush in should Jeevnathan attempt to harm the don.

Soon after they were seated, Raghupati, dressed in a long, full-sleeve white kurta and white dhoti, walked into the room. Jeev got up to shake Raghupati's hand and thanked him for agreeing to meet him. Raghupati said nothing, his expression hidden behind the gold-rimmed Ray-Bans he was wearing. He was tall, with a proud bearing, very fair and had a thick crop of black hair. He hardly looked an outlaw. He was guarded by eight muscular individuals armed with AK-47s and semi-automatic rifles. Four unarmed persons entered from the front door after a few seconds. The don sat on the largest sofa in the room, flanked by two of his unarmed guards. The rest of them took up positions behind him, near the doors and windows. Jeev and Bipin sat in the two armchairs facing the big sofa.

'I avoid meeting officials but I agreed to see you because of Bipinji's insistence,' Raghupati began. 'Let me make it clear that I will neither share any information nor will I become your source.' His voice was gruff and deep, incongruous with his soft face.

'I have not travelled all the way from Delhi to recruit you as a source or to obtain information; I only wish to discuss something with you. However, what I have to say is of a very sensitive nature. I cannot disclose it in the presence of either your guards or Bipin,' Jeevnathan said.

There was pin drop silence in the room. Raghupati looked calculatingly at Jeev for a long moment, then leaned back and whispered something to a henchman standing right behind him. The man left but returned soon with a revolver and stungun, which he handed to the don. The latter checked to ensure that they were fully loaded, apparently to warn Jeev against trying anything, and kept them on the centre table within his easy reach. Thereafter,

he instructed everyone to leave. Jeev breathed a sigh of relief and asked Bipin to wait for him in the car.

'You may be aware that we are not allowing any goods to go from India to Nepal,' Jeev began as soon as the two of them were alone in the room. 'We had to impose the economic blockade,' he explained, 'to force the king to abandon his policy of harbouring terrorists from Pakistan and prevent him from buying weapons from China that can later be used against us. But our efforts to make the king realize his folly in pursuing anti-India policies are not succeeding, despite starving Nepal of supplies of essential commodities. We believe that smugglers, operating on both sides of the border, have kept the flow of goods and fuel going. If the king holds on for even one more week, we suspect Chinese supplies will start flowing into Nepal on a massive scale. That will give Kathmandu the confidence to turn away from us forever and will convert Nepal into one of China's client states, just like Pakistan.' Jeev tried to put across the situation as succinctly as possible.

'Why are you telling me all this?' Raghupati asked.

'We believe that if the smuggling in your area stops for just five or six days, the reserves of fuel and food in Nepal will dry up, forcing the king to realize his foolhardiness. He may then be willing to listen to us and stop sheltering Pakistani terrorists, among other things,' Jeev explained.

'Who do you think I am? A smuggler?' snapped Raghupati.

'I am told you are a very influential man in this area and people know you as a Samaritan who helps those in need. Bipin told me that the poor look upon you as God. This time, it is your country that is in distress and needs your help,' Jeev argued persuasively.

'Even if I do have some influence in this area, what makes you think the smugglers will listen to me? The economic blockade has been a windfall for them. They are earning seventy to eighty lakh rupees a day. If they stop their activities for five days, they will stand to lose approximately four crores. I doubt if they will be willing to forego this huge sum for your national cause,' Raghupati responded.

'I cannot offer you a rupee to compensate their losses,' Jeev said. 'I can only ask you to think of your country's future, for which your grandfather fought and suffered during India's freedom movement,' Jeev appealed to him, trying to play on the don's ancestral pride.

'Who cares about the country these days? What matters is money and the power that you wield. You talk like my school teacher who fought for Gandhian principles but died in poverty. Besides, without the connivance of the civil administration, local police, immigration and customs officials, smugglers cannot operate on this scale. These officials and their political bosses are not going to allow the smugglers to stop,' Raghupati argued.

'Please, think it over. I know it will be an uphill task to choke the irregular supply of goods, but there is no one else whom I can turn to for help,' Jeev said.

Raghupati was silent for a while. Jeev couldn't tell what he was thinking as the sunglasses masked his expression.

'Very well, I will speak to them,' he finally agreed. 'But you have to promise that our meeting will remain a secret and our conversation will not be shared with anyone.'

'You have my solemn word.'

'The most I can hope to do is to persuade them to suspend smuggling operations for five to six days. If you are unable

to force the king to relent during this period, then don't come back to me,' Raghupati said.

'I won't.'

'You also have to give me a commitment that you will offer no excuses whenever I wish to meet you,' Raghupati said. A shrewd operator, he realized that knowing an intelligence officer, and that too a Brahmin, could be useful.

'My wife and daughter will be happy to meet you, but do not contact me through anyone, not even Bipin. I will give you a number. Call me directly on that,' Jeev said.

This was his subtle way of showing Raghupati that he was placing his trust in him. He wrote a number on a piece of paper.

As Jeev handed the slip to him, Raghupati asked with a smile, 'Tell me, did my man scare you when he brought the revolver and rifle and placed them on the table in front of you?'

'No. I have heard that you target only those who harm your interests. I knew that you would gain nothing by killing an unarmed intelligence officer who was walking into the lion's den without informing even his wife,' Jeev said.

'But aren't you harming my interests by asking me to suspend my smuggling operations?' Raghupati countered light-heartedly, indicating for the first time that he was directly involved in orchestrating the smuggling operations.

'Well, in one sense that may be true. But if you reflect on it, you will realize that you are doing something in the interest of your country. You are only emulating your grandfather who sacrificed his life for this country during the Quit India Movement in 1942.'

'I don't think people today even know what the Quit India Movement was all about. Anyway, since we are talking about interests, I have one particular desire that perhaps you will be able to help me achieve.'

Jeev looked at him enquiringly.

'You spoke of service to the nation. I feel I can contribute by becoming a minister,' Raghupati trailed off meaningfully.

'I work for India's foreign intelligence service and have nothing to do with Indian politics. I can make you a minister in Nepal but not here,' Jeev said. 'I'm afraid you may have over-estimated my abilities,' Jeev said.

'I find you to be a very selfish person. You seem to believe in only taking help but not giving anything in return,' Raghupati said softly, while fiddling with the revolver.

Jeev kept quiet, unwilling to enter into a pointless conversation. With nothing further to discuss, he stood up to take his leave of the don.

Raghupati, however, insisted that Jeev join him for dinner. Not wanting to offend the don in any way, Jeev agreed.

Raghupati led him to a room at the other end of the veranda. It had no furniture but was spotlessly clean. Two mats were spread out on the floor. In front of each was placed a large plate and several small bowls, all made of silver.

'I don't know why you took this trouble. Bipin has already made arrangements for my dinner,' Jeev said.

'You are a special guest. Besides, you are a Brahmin. How can I let you go without offering you a home-made meal?' Raghupati said.

As they sat on the mats, two persons came forward and served them food, carefully filling each bowl with a different

preparation. It was an excellent vegetarian meal, cooked in home-made butter.

After dinner, which Jeev had enjoyed thoroughly, he gave a thousand rupees each to the cook and two bearers and presented Raghupati with a sari for his wife and a pashmina shawl for himself. Raghupati seemed pleased with the expensive gifts as he threw the shawl across his shoulders.

'I have to tell you something,' Jeev confessed as Raghupati was walking with him towards the car. 'I am neither the deputy chief of the Agency nor is my name Amulya Tripathi. I actually head the Eastern Service Bureau in Lucknow and my name is Jeevnathan. But the telephone number that I gave you is genuine.'

'I knew it all along. But you are a Brahmin all the same,' Raghupati said.

Both smiled.

As Jeev was driven off, he glanced in the rear-view mirror and saw Raghupati slowly walking back to the house, surrounded again by his bodyguards.

When Jeev arrived at Bipin's house, he apologized to his wife and told her that he had already had dinner and asked for tea. An hour later, he left for Lucknow. En route, he kept wondering whether he had done the right thing in exposing his cover to a mafia leader, when their discussion had seemed to be going so well. He was not sure whether it had been necessary for him to go to the extent that he had to reassure the don that he was dealing with an honest man. Finally, exhausted, he fell into a fitful sleep as the car bumped and jolted its way over the roads.

Jeev reached Lucknow at 6.00 a.m., went straight to bed and fell into a deep sleep. Five hours later, he woke up, got dressed and called Rajan.

'Sir, I met the subject last night. He did not commit to anything, but I am hopeful,' Jeev reported.

'I am sure it will work,' Rajan said and hung up.

'What bravado are you up to? The driver told me that you had gone to meet a criminal, unarmed and without a police escort. He was nervous and kept praying for your life till you came out of the house,' Manini, who had overheard his conversation with Rajan, asked sharply.

'Don't you know that we deal mostly with criminals, war lords, terrorists, saboteurs and traitors?' Jeev asked, smiling.

'No wonder the Agency's officers look so hardened and shifty. But apart from being an Agency officer, you are also my husband and a father,' she chided.

'I have invited this particular criminal over for dinner to our house and have promised to introduce him to you and Adya,' Jeev said calmly.

'I'm not surprised,' Manini retorted. 'Other officers introduce their family members to eminent persons from honourable disciplines like art, literature and music, and here is my dear husband, inviting a criminal to dine with us.'

Jeev merely smiled, letting her jibe pass.

Fifty-two hours later, reports from the field units indicated a steep drop in the smuggling of essential commodities into Nepal and desperate attempts by Nepalese authorities to contact the Indian smugglers. With official check-posts already sealed and a large number of unauthorized routes remaining dry, the reserves of fuel and food dropped alarmingly. On the eleventh day of the blockade, the king offered to talk to Delhi on a whole range of bilateral issues in a spirit of accommodation. India responded by lifting the economic blockade.

Rajan called to thank Jeev for a job well done. Jeev wanted to contact Raghupati to express his gratitude, but he knew it wouldn't be prudent to do so on the phone. He toyed with the idea of travelling to Gorakhpur to meet Raghupati and even asked Bipin to set up a meeting with him. But the don was not available. Busy with finalizing the plan to wind up the bureau's operations, Jeev nonetheless waited anxiously for Raghupati to contact him, but the don never called. Perhaps Raghupati felt that Jeev was of no use to him in fulfilling his ministerial ambitions. Or maybe he did not want to create problems for a fellow Brahmin who was serving in a sensitive department of the government. In any event, Raghupati's silence was just one more loss of an exciting contact. Jeev had had several such breaks from some of his finest sources with whom he had worked closely for years, for reasons that remained forever inexplicable.

In the days following the lifting of the blockade, the information coming in from the field units reduced to a trickle. The few reports that were being received from leftover operations were sketchy and referred mostly to sporadic clashes between the police and the Maoists. Others reported on attempts by the opposition political parties to revive their movement for the restoration of democracy in Nepal, which had been put on the back burner due to the blockade.

Meanwhile, preparations for the closure of the ESB continued. Three weeks after the economic sanctions against Nepal were lifted, Jeevnathan left on a ten-day tour of the four sub-bureaus located in the north-eastern hills of

Uttar Pradesh to assess their logistical needs before arriving at a practical time schedule for their closure.

On the last leg of his tour to the Kheri sub-bureau, Jeev reached the local guest house of the forest department in the evening. After he freshened up and had tea, the officer in charge of the sub-bureau handed him a copy of the following day's programme and a cryptic message, received earlier that day from the telecommunication officer in Lucknow. It noted that Alok Raut wanted Jeevnathan to visit Jogbani urgently. After dinner, Jeev went to the sub-bureau office from where he tried several times to contact Alok on the phone, but was unable to get through to him, despite booking lightning calls. Apparently, the phone lines had been snapped at several places due to landslides and were not likely to be repaired for the next two to three days. He then tried to send a message through the Agency's communication links but failed. Frustrated, he cut short his visit and left the following day after an early breakfast, driving for ten hours straight to reach Lucknow at six in the evening.

The following day, Jeev took a flight to Patna, from where he drove for another nine hours to reach the sub-bureau office in Jogbani by 9.00 p.m. Alok, who was at home having dinner, was taken completely by surprise when the guard from the office came rushing in to inform him of Jeev's arrival. With communications and roads being what they were, he hadn't expected him for another week. Taken aback by Jeev's quick response, Alok quickly spoke to the resident engineer of the irrigation department and secured a room in their dak bungalow for Jeev. He then hurried to the office to meet Jeev and escort him to the bungalow.

For a building that had been constructed during British times, it appeared well maintained. Jeev's room was fairly large with a wooden floor, high ceiling and four huge windows. There was, however, no fan. It was dominated by a massive, king-sized bed over which was draped a mosquito net. A stone-paved veranda ran along two sides of the room. The lighting inside the room and on the veranda was very poor due to the low voltage and the area around the building, dotted with shrubs and trees, was shrouded in darkness. As Jeev went inside to unpack, the caretaker brought out a Petromax lamp to brighten the veranda.

After a quick wash, Jeev came out to join Alok, who had been waiting for him on the veranda. He pulled up a cane chair and sat down facing him. 'What was it that you wanted me to be here for so urgently?' he asked.

'Sir, I recently met a senior member of the standing committee of the Communist Party of Nepal through one of my part-time Nepalese contacts and had the opportunity to hear his views on the current political situation in Nepal. I thought he could be a valuable asset for us, but I didn't want to go ahead unless you met him and assessed his true potential,' Alok replied.

'What exactly is his role in the party?'

'Apart from influencing most political decisions, he draws his real strength from being the number two in the party's military commission and virtually runs the armed cadre. He is extremely secretive and speaks mostly in Maoist jargon. He keeps harping on the fact that Delhi has joined hands with the king and the Nepali Congress to suppress the people's war, threatening that he will never forgive the Indian leadership for this,' Alok reported.

'If he is so hostile, how come he agreed to meet me?' Jeev probed.

'Sir, it wasn't easy to convince him. Initially, he refused point blank to meet anyone from India, but in subsequent meetings, he wasn't so dismissive.'

'Did he give any hint that he had met someone from the Agency before?' Jeev asked.

'Sir, I did ask him about that, but he neither denied nor confirmed it. He firmly believes that the Indian Army and intelligence agencies are advising the Royal Nepalese Army, the Royal Intelligence Bureau and the National Investigation Department on how to crush the Maoist movement. After a lot of persuasion by Tirtha and myself, he agreed to meet you only once and that too on Nepali soil. Before he developed cold feet or changed his mind, I thought of apprising you of the development and sent that cable,' Alok explained.

'Who is Tirtha?'

'Sir, he is a school teacher. I met him through a contact and we have since become good friends. He is the Maoist leader's most trusted comrade in the area and his house is the only place in the village where the leader will stay. After the meeting in which you challenged us to search for wonders, I began hounding Tirtha to introduce me to his leader. Finally, three weeks ago, I met him for the first time. Since then we have met four times.'

'But I have not seen any report on your meetings.'

'Sir, there was nothing of substance that I could report. Our conversations were largely one-sided, with him holding forth. He would treat me as his captive audience and give long discourses on his party's Maoist ideology. He wasn't interested in hearing anything that I had to say.

On the day I sent you the message, he was in Tirtha's house, which is in Rani village, right across our post. Tirtha sent word to me, and I rushed to meet him. As usual, he began by talking about his vision of establishing a classless society in Nepal and building its economy and defence on the Chinese model, shaped by Mao. But then he surprised me by asking me to arrange a meeting with you as early as possible, on the condition that you meet him in Tirtha's house. I could hardly believe this breakthrough in tapping such an important target and cabled you immediately,' Alok said.

Jeev, who had been listening carefully to Alok's recounting, had a feeling he knew who this mysterious leader was. 'It sounds like the leader you are referring to is Kamal Aryal,' Jeev said.

'Yes, sir,' Alok, looking a little surprised, confirmed his suspicions.

Jeev could hardly believe his luck. Alok had indeed performed wonders. Nonetheless, he had to proceed with extreme caution.

'I don't think it is advisable for me to visit him clandestinely in Rani. He is likely to be under the intense surveillance of the National Investigation Department. If I get caught meeting him, it will cause major embarrassment for the Agency,' Jeev said.

'Sir, I can try to persuade him to come here and meet you,' Alok said.

'Even if I do take the risk of meeting him on Nepalese soil, the important thing to consider is how we will sustain the relationship. I cannot be his handler, as it won't be possible for me to travel here frequently to brief him. I could have asked you to operate him, but you have completed your tenure in the bureau and are likely to be transferred

out soon. I could persuade headquarters to run him as one of their high-grade operations, but given his apathy towards the Agency, I doubt that he will agree to such an arrangement,' Jeev opined.

'Sir, he will not agree to meet anyone else,' Alok said.

'But why me?'

'I told him that you were very close to the prime minister and were his principal advisor on all matters pertaining to Nepal,' Alok said timidly.

'But that is not true. Anyway, where is he now?' Jeev enquired.

'Sir, I will have to check with Tirtha. He is on the move most of the time, to motivate his political and military volunteers.'

'Having come this far, I think I will take a chance. Find out if Aryal is in Rani. If he is, I will go and meet him. He is too good a prospect to be ignored,' Jeev said.

Alok left the guest house after a late dinner. Tired after his long journey, Jeev hit the bed and immediately fell asleep.

With no time to waste, Alok headed straight for Tirtha's modest house in Rani. The forty-five-minute walk took him across the Parmar River. He got there after midnight. Luckily, Tirtha was awake.

'What brings you here at this late hour?' Tirtha asked, surprised to see Alok at his doorstep.

'My boss arrived in Jogbani earlier this evening. He wants to know if the meeting can be organized in the next forty-eight hours,' Alok explained.

'It is short notice, but it may be possible. Stay here and rest. Meanwhile, I'll go talk to a couple of underground

volunteers who are also in Rani to find out where he could possibly be now,' Tirtha said as he slipped on his shoes. He locked the house from outside to waylay the police patrol and left.

On his return at 4.00 a.m., he told an anxious Alok that he had sent couriers to contact the leader with the message that a senior officer from the Agency was camping in Jogbani and wanted to meet him, and the officer expected a response by that very evening.

Alok left Rani at 5.00 a.m. and went straight to the dak bungalow to brief Jeev.

With nothing much to do but wait, Jeev spent the morning speaking to the employees of the sub-bureau and listening to the problems that they were likely to face following closure of the bureau. He spent the afternoon relaxing. For the second successive day, he remained cut off from the rest of the world, as the P&T and Agency's lines were down.

The courier returned with good news. Aryal had agreed to meet Jeev at 11.00 p.m., but only at Tirtha's house. Jeev was not comfortable with the choice of venue and asked Alok to make one last attempt to persuade the leader to come to Jogbani.

'Tell him that if I happen to be seen and detained by the Nepalese police, it will not only expose both of us but also finish our respective careers,' he said. 'Also, assure him that no one other than me will have a glimpse of him on this side of the border.'

Alok did not look forward to what he knew would be a very difficult conversation, but he also knew he had to try. It was an uphill task, but with the help of Tirtha and all his skills of persuasion, he managed to convince the leader to

accompany him to the dak bungalow in Jogbani. He also had to make a commitment that Tirtha would remain by Aryal's side throughout.

Jeev waited for Alok on the veranda under the dim light of two kerosene lamps, reading a book on how to be politically correct. There had been no electricity in the town since that afternoon, and if the caretaker was to be believed, it was not likely to be restored before the next day. With the moon still a couple of hours away from appearing, the area beyond the veranda was enveloped in darkness, relieved only by the twinkling of fireflies. Suddenly, he heard the wooden gate creaking open. As he looked up, he saw Alok emerging out of the darkness, walking towards him followed by two men—no doubt Aryal and Tirtha.

After a brief and formal introduction of the visitors, Alok excused himself, saying that he had to go make arrangements for their dinner. Jeev nodded and asked Aryal whether his associate could sit in the adjoining room so that they could talk in confidence. Before Aryal could say anything, Tirtha volunteered to go out and assist Alok. He later confided to Alok that he had felt it would be best if their meeting remained private, lest his presence prevented his leader from conceding grounds and entering into a secret relationship for the benefit of the people's war.

Jeev was struck by Aryal's rustic appearance. His face had the rugged look of someone who spent much of their time in jungles and bunkers. His build was sturdy and he was of medium height. He had a thick crop of black hair, an untrimmed moustache that hid his lips, and bushy eyebrows. He was wearing dark grey trousers and a crumpled white half-sleeve shirt.

'I am grateful that you could find some time to meet me here,' Jeev began.

Aryal said nothing.

'Alok has been telling me that you are quite hopeful of establishing a people's democracy in Nepal in the very near future,' Jeev deliberately chose a topic that he hoped would put the leader at ease. Hesitation and suspicion were typical of all sources meeting their handlers for the first time. This was more evident in the case of those who belonged to terrorist, insurgent and ideologically violent organizations.

'I don't know when this will be possible but yes, this has definitely been our dream for a long time,' Aryal said.

'Have you reached any understanding with other leftist and mainstream political parties to jointly step up the struggle to realize this dream?' Jeev asked.

Aryal remained silent, as yet unsure of whether he should open up on these matters to an officer from the Agency whom he had yet to get to know.

'You may be wondering why I came to see you,' Jeev pressed. 'My purpose is to have some clarity from you regarding whether you have decided to fight alone for your kind of democracy or for democracy that is acceptable to other political parties,' he asked.

'I cannot work as your source and share details of our programmes, policies and the state of preparedness of our armed cadres and political activists,' Aryal frowned.

'I am not here to recruit you as a source. Because of your standing in the party, it would be foolish of me to expect that you will meet me regularly or reveal your party's secret activities. It is not feasible for both of us to enter into the conventional relationship that usually exists between a source and his intelligence operative,' he emphasized.

'You surely haven't come here to shake my hand and have dinner with me?' Aryal punched.

'You are right. I have actually come to seek your help in overthrowing the king,' Jeev said calmly.

Aryal stared at him. 'Why?'

'With each passing day, he is becoming more and more ruthless in suppressing opposition to his regime by employing the brute force of the Royal Nepalese Army and the police. He is using a discredited Panchayati government, which he foisted on Nepal and filled with his loyalists, cronies and henchmen, to treat you as slaves and seems adamant on not allowing any democratic institution to take root in your country,' he added.

'We are aware of this and already have a plan. We are raising an underground people's army that will decimate the Royal Nepalese Army and force the king to abandon his crumbling throne,' Aryal claimed. 'I don't think we need to work with you,' he opined.

'I don't know if you have drawn up a time-bound plan of action to achieve this objective. But I firmly believe that if you travel alone on this difficult and dangerous journey, it will take years for you to reach your goal. I think you should work with the nationalist and mainstream political parties to jointly organize a massive and sustained movement, if you really want to blow away the king's rule in a flash like the Romanians did to Nicolae Ceausescu,' Jeev stressed, leading the discussion to his main agenda.

'We are already in contact with the Nepalese Congress,' Aryal began opening up, 'but we are very sceptical about their sincerity in joining our battle against the king. It is a party full of fossils and opportunists. Since they have benefitted all these years from the king's so-called heavenly

order, they cannot think of a regime without the king heading it. On the contrary, my cadres are young and imbued with Mao's revolutionary ideas. They are not prepared to accept the king in any role in the new political dispensation. They want his severed head and a forcible end to his years of tyrannical rule. I don't think we can ever have a meeting point with these reactionary nationalist parties on this issue,' he argued.

'I value your judgment, but why don't you consider adopting a different strategy?' Jeev argued. 'A Maoist strategy to overwhelm the king may not work because before that, you will have to decimate the so-called reactionaries, the party workers of the Nepali congress, the Madhesis and the king's loyalists, all of whom are deeply entrenched in your political system and are huge in numbers,' Jeev argued.

'So what do you suggest we do?' Aryal probed.

'A better option will be to approach your ultimate objective step by step. First, get democracy restored, in whichever package it comes in. Then, once you have a firm foothold in the government, wage a violent struggle to clip the king's wings. Tolerate him as a ceremonial head during the interim period only as a tactical move, but when the constitution is drafted, insist on a republic. I am sure that if you seek a vote for a republic, you will win hands down in any election. And then you can dispense with the king altogether,' Jeev explained.

'But why are you so concerned whether we are ruled by a king or live in a people's democracy?' Aryal questioned.

'Our reasons may be different, but we both want to remove the king. Like you, we also believe that a monarch cannot always be trusted to look after the welfare of

his people. We also believe that only a democracy can be genuinely responsive to our economic and security concerns,' Jeev pointed out.

'How can you be sure that the Nepalese Congress or our party will take a position that is any different from the king's when it comes to acceding to your demands on bilateral issues, which have always been unfavourable to our sovereign interests?' Aryal asked.

'At least we will have the option of arguing our case before a larger audience and will not be dictated by a maverick who thinks that he is divine but acts like a demon.'

'You have given me a lot to think about,' Aryal said softly. 'While I have absolutely no doubt that India will push any new government hard to further its own agenda, at least for now we share a common goal. Perhaps we can work together after all. Let me go back and talk to my armed cadres and members of the Standing Committee and Politburo. If they approve of your idea, I will talk to the leaders of other political parties about launching a joint movement.'

'I also have a specific action plan for you. I want you to organize violent demonstrations simultaneously at three places and sustain them for forty-eight hours. The agitators are bound to face a violent response from the police and the RNA and suffer casualties, but you have to ensure that their repression does not deter more activists from joining the protests and the mayhem continues unabated,' Jeev outlined his ideas.

'It's a bad plan,' Aryal remarked. 'You cannot throw out a well-entrenched autocratic ruler by holding a few violent demonstrations. And why do you insist on sustaining the violence only for two days?' he asked.

'Because the news of protestors' deaths at the hands of the police will take that much time to spread to other parts of the country, prompting people to come out onto the streets in large numbers to demand swift punishment and justice. Since the government will not concede any ground to the agitators, the violence will snowball into massive protests, forcing the government to fall,' Jeev explained.

'What is the guarantee that other political parties, student and labour groups will jump into the fray?' Aryal asked.

'Let's not get distracted by what may or may not happen. One can never predict the course of a revolution. But I can sense its imminent possibility. I came to Jogbani looking for a spark to ignite the fuel for change. I firmly believe that you are that spark. Trust me, there is history to support my contention. Once the protest erupts, it will spread like wildfire, reducing the king's dictatorial regime to ashes,' Jeev deliberately spoke with passion.

'I am still not convinced that a few protests can bring down the monarchy. But since you appear confident, I will accept your plan. However, it will require resources, which we do not have. Will you be able to provide us with the funds?'

Jeev was surprised by Aryal's candid request.

'How much will you need?' he asked.

'Seventy-five thousand Indian rupees to start with. Then another seventy-five thousand can be sent through Tirtha after a fortnight,' Aryal said without batting an eyelid.

'Give me twenty-four hours to arrange the amount.'

'All right. Give the money to Tirtha. He will make sure it is delivered to me. He is one of my most trusted comrades,' Aryal said.

Jeev nodded his agreement and Aryal stood up to leave.

'It's late. I must get back,' he said.

He still did not know Jeevnathan's name nor did he think it necessary to ask, for he knew that intelligence officers never revealed their real names to contacts.

'Please stay for dinner,' Jeev invited him.

Aryal agreed.

It was 11.30 p.m. by then. Both moved to the dining hall and sat on the hard wooden chairs placed around an oval table. On Jeev's insistence, Alok and Tirtha also joined them.

After the simple meal of rice, goat meat and salad, Aryal left along with Tirtha. Jeev accompanied them up to the riverbank on the Indian side of the border. It was a moonlit night and they did not need anything to light their path.

'When and where do we meet next?' Jeev asked.

'I don't know. Maybe never, but I will try to be in touch with you through Tirtha,' Aryal responded. He paused before continuing, 'If for some reason my boys fail to pull off your plan, do not think that I betrayed you,' he said seriously.

'No, I won't. I know you will do your best,' Jeev replied.

'I don't know why, but I have begun to believe that your plan may work as a catalyst for bigger political upheavals.'

They shook hands warmly before Aryal and Tirtha set off to cross the river that informally demarcated the border. Jeev stood on the riverbank till the leader was lost in the early morning fog. When he returned to the dak bungalow, it was 4.30 a.m.

What Kamal Aryal had asked for was too big an amount for Jeev's comfort. He neither carried so much money nor had the power to sanction payments of over a thousand rupees.

He tried to contact Naveen through the Agency's dedicated communication link to obtain his approval in principle, but the link was down. In desperation, he took a gamble. After breakfast, he drove to Muzaffarpur to borrow money from one of his relatives. Although surprised and curious about Jeev's sudden appearance and request, the relative handed over the money in private without asking any questions. Relieved, Jeev joined him and his family for lunch, returning to Jogbani late in the evening.

That same night, Alok left for Tirtha's house to deliver the money, but Aryal had left by then. However, Tirtha told him to stay the night as Aryal would be back the following morning.

At six the next morning, Alok woke up to the sound of the Marxist leader talking to a group of young volunteers in the adjoining room. Seeing that Alok was awake, Tirtha told him that the leader was addressing the new recruits of the area and would be spending the whole day in the house, leaving that night for Rolpa. During the day, no one would enter or leave the house except for him so that the agents of the National Investigation Department did not suspect the leader's presence in the village.

'Do I then remain confined to the house for the rest of the day?' Alok enquired.

'Don't worry. I will arrange a safe exit for you before noon,' Tirtha said and went to inform the leader that Alok was awake.

Aryal greeted Alok warmly, and the latter handed him the money. Aryal counted the amount, put it in a small cotton pouch and tucked it inside his trousers.

'Please tell your boss that if I fail to execute his plan, I will not return the money, but I will also not ask for further payments,' the leader said.

Curious about the plan, but knowing he couldn't ask any questions, Alok merely nodded. Aryal quickly hugged Alok before returning to the group of young recruits.

To avoid the watchful eyes of the National Investigation Department, Tirtha escorted Alok back to the border through a circuitous route often used by Aryal's men.

As soon as Jeev returned to Lucknow, he sent a cable to Naveen, briefing him on his meeting with Kamal Aryal. He named the operation 'Bandicoot'. Three days later, Naveen replied. The Chief had been told about the operation, and he felt that the objective set for Bandicoot was unrealistic and the amount that was proposed to be invested in an untested source was disproportionate to the task. The Chief had also taken a dim view of Jeev's unilateral decision to pay the large sum of seventy-five thousand rupees without first consulting headquarters. If Jeev was still keen on exploiting Bandicoot's potential, then he could run him as a source of information on a salary of one thousand rupees per month.

Jeevnathan was aghast. He immediately contacted Naveen and asked him if Rajan had seen his cable.

'Not yet. He is on tour and will be back early next week,' Naveen said.

'I am surprised the Chief cannot see the long term-benefits of this operation. Maybe he wasn't briefed properly,' Jeev said, the reproach clear in his tone. 'I would rather give up Bandicoot than run him as a source. In any case, the bureau is going to be wound up soon, so why add a load to an already sinking ship,' he remarked caustically.

'You're right, just dump him and focus on wrapping up the bureau's operations,' Naveen suggested.

'Maybe. In any case, please reimburse the money before I leave Lucknow. I have to pay off the loan I took to pay Bandicoot,' Jeev said.

'Let Rajan return. I will ask him to persuade the Chief to sanction the amount as a one-time exception. It would have been easier for Rajan to reimburse the expenditure if you had split the payment, keeping the amounts within his financial powers,' Naveen pointed out.

'I won't resort to such manipulations. I have done nothing wrong. I spent the money for a cause that I believe is a worthwhile one.'

The phone line went dead before Naveen could say anything. Jeev felt relieved. He did not want to discuss the matter further with Naveen. He was more interested in waiting to hear what Rajan had to say on his discussions with Aryal. He was confident that Rajan would be excited at the prospect and sanction the amount. It would be unwise to pull out after pushing Aryal to agree to execute a plan that could have far-reaching political consequences for both Nepal and India, he thought.

Thirty-six hours later, Jeevnathan was a happy man. Rajan called and asked him to keep pursuing the Bandicoot and not to worry about its financial implications.

A couple of days later, his backache returned after almost six months to lay Jeevnathan low. He could not go into the office. Deputy Awasthy came to his home every evening to brief him on the day's communications received from headquarters and the sub-bureaus and the replies that he had sent. Finally feeling better after resting for the whole week, Jeev went to the office. After disposing of pending

papers and dictating a letter for Naveen updating him on the preparations made for the withdrawal of personnel from the sub-bureaus, he began going through the cables that were meant to be seen only by him. A cable from the Patan sub-bureau struck him as interesting. It was from Vidyadhar Banerjee. Characteristically, he seemed to have written after a lot of hesitation. The tenor was exhaustively respectful and apologetic. In the entire twenty-line cable, the actual substance was mentioned in one sentence. He wrote that one of his contacts had promised to introduce him to a national-level leader of the Nepali Congress and that the meeting could take place any day. However, there was no mention of what he wanted Jeevnathan to do. Intrigued, Jeev wrote back, directing Vidyadhar to meet him immediately.

That evening, his backache persisting, Jeev had an early dinner and retired to bed. Manini settled down in the living room to watch the 9.00 p.m. Doordarshan news. Suddenly, she heard the sentry arguing with someone outside. As the conversation became louder, she came out and asked the guard what the raised voices were about.

'I am sorry, ma'am. An officer from the Patan sub-bureau is here and he insists on meeting sir. I told him to come back in the morning, but he won't listen. He says that he has been summoned by sir and won't leave without meeting him.'

'Where is he?'

'He is standing outside, ma'am,' the guard said.

'Let me check if Jeev is awake.'

Jeev was reading a book.

'Did you ask an officer from Patan to come see you urgently at this odd hour?' she enquired.

'Why?'

'He is standing outside the house.'

'Did he say his name was Vidyadhar?'

'I haven't spoken to him. The guard told me that the officer insists on meeting you before he returns to Patan,' she said.

Jeev struggled to his feet and walked out to the gate. 'Where is he?'

A man stepped forward out of the shadows. It was Vidyadhar. He stood there uncertainly, looking scared, as if expecting to be severely reprimanded at any moment. He greeted Jeev meekly and stood still, his head drooping over his chest as if he was about to be hanged.

'Vidyadhar? I didn't expect you so soon. Come inside,' Jeev said and led him into the living room.

'Sir, I know it's very late, but I didn't want to wait till the morning…' he trailed off, looking uncertain again.

'Do you have a place to stay for the night?' Jeev enquired as they settled down in the living room.

'No sir, I will take a late-night bus back to Patan,' Vidyadhar replied, looking down at the floor.

Jeev phoned the caretaker of the bureau's guest house and instructed him to provide dinner and a room for Vidyadhar.

'Now, who is this contact of yours?' Jeev asked after adjusting his back against a pillow.

'Sir, he is a cousin of the Nepali Congress leader Govind. He told me that Govind would be willing to meet anyone from India who could assist him in bringing democracy back on the rails in Nepal. But the person, he insists, must be an important official or an influential politician and must enjoy the confidence of the Indian prime minister,' Vidyadhar said.

'How did you meet this cousin?' Jeev probed.

'After you challenged us to raise top-level sources, I sought the help of a low-level member of the Nepali Congress who has been working for us as a source for the past several years. He told me that he knew a cousin of Govind and could arrange a meeting with him. Subsequently, we visited Kathmandu where I was introduced to the cousin as a senior officer of the Agency. The meeting lasted only ten minutes as he had another appointment. But three days later, the cousin sent me a message through the source that he would like to meet me in Kathmandu at the earliest. This time our meeting was exclusive. I briefed him about your background and told him that you would be interested in meeting Govind. When he asked why you wanted to meet him, I told him that it had something to do with an important political mission, but that I couldn't give him any more details because I was not privy to what you wanted to discuss,' Vidyadhar said.

'Why did you not try to meet Govind?' Jeev asked.

Looking uncomfortable, Vidyadhar said, 'Sir, I was very nervous because I had gone to Kathmandu without your approval. I wanted to leave from there as fast as possible. I was also not sure if I could properly handle an asset of Govind's stature. Sir, I don't have the experience to interact with politicians of his standing. Besides, as the cousin mentioned, Govind is only interested in meeting a senior official or influential politician. I didn't want to ruin any chances we had by suggesting that I meet him.'

'Please ask the cousin to fix my meeting with Govind at any place of his choosing in India. You have already hinted at why I want to meet him. If he insists again on knowing what I wish to discuss, tell him that I will disclose the details to Govind during our meeting,' Jeev said.

'Sir.'

Jeev got up, indicating that the discussion was over.

'Let me know as soon as the meeting is confirmed.'

'Sir.'

Jeev led Vidyadhar out to the veranda, called for the driver and asked him to drop him at the guest house.

'How is your back pain?' Manini enquired as Jeev lay down.

'Manageable,' he said and rolled over to his left side.

'It will get worse if you don't rest for a few more days. I know you suffer from an exalted sense of duty towards the nation's security, but keep that on hold till you recover fully. Why do you forget that the Chief has sent you here to enjoy yourself and wind up the set-up?'

'You are right. I'll plan a holiday to Nainital for us. Adya's exams will be over soon and Maitri will also be joining us next week for her vacation.'

'Don't lie before sleeping. It invites bad dreams,' Manini jibed.

Jeev, however, went to bed with a smile on his face. The Eastern Service Bureau was turning out to be an asset to the Agency after all.

A week later Jeev received a cable from Vidyadhar that Govind had agreed to meet him in Varanasi on the following day at 10.00 a.m. Jeev was to contact the cousin on 2364571 to get directions to the meeting place. Jeev immediately booked a lightning call to Naveen to apprise him of the impending meeting and check whether anyone in the Agency had met or handled Govind earlier. But Naveen

was away on an assignment. Jeev then rang up Rajan and sought his advice.

'How does it matter whether someone has met him or not?' Rajan asked. 'You go ahead and meet him. He may be more forthright and honest in talking to you. He has so far been wary of our recent overtures. For your information, he is quite overbearing and does not easily accept contrary views. Nevertheless, he is a critical cog in our scheme of things.'

'Would you like me to discuss any particular issue with him?' Jeev asked.

'Meet him with an open mind. It is better that you don't go with a brief. Let the dialogue evolve naturally. In any case, you know what the current political situation is and what we expect from him. The time to strike is now and he can be of great value in driving home the advantage of the simmering discontent,' Rajan pointed out.

'Sir, I will let you know how the meeting goes,' Jeev promised before ringing off.

Jeev drove the whole night to reach Varanasi in the early hours of the following morning. Seeing her father in discomfort due to back pain, Maitri, a third-year medical student, had insisted on accompanying him, ignoring his objections. Jeev went straight to the house of an old friend of his, a doctor. When his insistent knocking finally brought the doctor to the door, rubbing the sleep from his eyes, he was surprised to see Jeev and Maitri standing in front of him. Jeev smiled and told him that he had urgent business in Varanasi, and was hoping he could take advantage of

his friend's hospitality while he was there. Happy to see his old friend, the doctor led Jeev and Maitri to the guest bedroom so they could get some much-needed rest. After an hour's sound sleep, Jeev woke up somewhat refreshed and called Govind's cousin. He answered the phone almost immediately, speaking softly in British-accented English and gave Jeev the directions to the hotel where Govind was staying. Jeev got ready quickly and had a sumptuous breakfast with the doctor and his wife. The doctor noticed that Jeev was in pain and enquired about his symptoms. He gave Jeev some medicine and advised him to avoid returning to Lucknow by road. Jeev merely smiled and left for the meeting.

Jeev reached the hotel at around 9.00 a.m. and had no difficulty in identifying the cousin, who was waiting for him in the lobby, thanks to the physical description provided by Vidyadhar. They shook hands, but the cousin avoided making polite conversation. He merely said that the patriarch was waiting in his room and requested Jeev to follow him.

Govind greeted Jeev warmly. He was tall, handsome and dressed in a starched white dhoti and kurta. The demands of remaining in active politics had not affected the glow on his face.

'I was not very keen on meeting you, but my cousin was insistent,' he began. 'I have little faith in your Agency, which is notorious for flip-flopping with respect to its relationships with friends. You are trained perhaps to swim only with the tide. Your leadership works only for short-term gains. I met one of your chiefs long ago. He was only a senior officer then. I found him to be not only arrogant but also ill informed. As I feared, he turned out to be

thoroughly unreliable. He withdrew support to us as soon as his immediate interests were served. Subsequently, I met many of your senior officers, but they were no different. They had neither clout in the government nor the capacity to back their tall operational claims.'

Jeev remained silent, realizing it would be best to let the leader finish his rant before saying anything.

'What particularly annoys me,' Govind resumed his litany of complaints, 'is that your operational policies are shaped by individuals who are either not conversant with ground realities or cannot carry their seniors to back their ideas. And every time there is a change in your leadership, your priorities and nature of support also change, sometimes drastically, leaving your friends like me in the lurch.'

Govind paused to ring up room service and ordered three cups of tea before continuing. 'I assume you have been sent by your chief to gauge whether I am willing to fulfil yet another set of his demands for some immediate gain,' he stopped as someone came up to him to hand over an envelope and the morning newspapers. He opened the envelope, pulled out a folded sheet of paper and gave it to his cousin. Meanwhile, the room service waiter came in and served them tea.

'So tell me, what has prompted you to come here to meet me?' Govind finally asked.

'I know you will find this hard to believe, but I came only to see you and hear what you had to say on the current political developments in Nepal. Neither the Chief nor any senior officer has sent me with an agenda. As an intelligence officer looking after Nepal's affairs, I follow the events in your country closely. I thought of sharing my ideas on how the current situation can be turned to your favour. But more

importantly, I wanted to meet you because I had heard so much about your political sagacity and your unflinching faith in democracy,' Jeev said.

'And what are these ideas of yours?' Govind ignored Jeev's compliments.

'We all know that you are currently waging a political struggle against the king. But like all your previous attempts, this time also, your movement for the restoration of democracy may collapse and remain confined to merely holding a few demonstrations and protest meetings,' Jeev opined.

'So what do you think we should do, sit back and watch the king crush our movement?' Govind shot back.

'No, I am not asking you to run away. But I do believe that if political parties, students, teachers, lawyers, doctors and other sections of the society rise in revolt simultaneously and can sustain it for a fortnight, the movement has a reasonable chance of succeeding,' Jeev replied.

'I am already talking to the communists, students and other organized groups and working out a common minimum programme,' Govind interrupted.

'I am aware of that. But you cannot keep talking forever. A time limit has to be set. I think you should serve an ultimatum to the king that he must restore democracy within six weeks, failing which all of you will launch a fierce and decisive struggle till democracy is rescued from his clutches. To make him understand that your threat is real, all mainstream political parties will have to come together on a common platform and call jointly for an end to the king's rule and warn him of disastrous consequences should he refuse to relent,' Jeev explained.

'It's not so simple. Getting the various political parties and groups, which hold diametrically opposite views and objectives, together and making them come out on to the streets to protest simultaneously will be an uphill task. Just to give you an idea of how irreconcilable our political positions are, the king's loyalists in the Panchayati government are willing to join our movement but will do so only if the king is accorded a constitutional responsibility in any future political dispensation. The communists, on the other hand, are fiercely opposed to conceding any role to the king. Ideally, they want his severed head, but if that is not feasible, they will only settle for his final and complete exit from the palace,' Govind pointed out.

'I don't think you have to worry too much about the monarchists' participation. They will join your bandwagon once the struggle picks up momentum. It is the communists that you have to work on, as early as possible,' Jeev urged.

'I am also in touch with like-minded policemen and civil service employees,' Govind confided.

'You don't have to waste time on chameleons. They will switch their loyalty once they see the writing on the wall,' Jeev remarked.

Their discussion was interrupted as another round of tea and snacks was served. Govind took the opportunity to enquire about Jeev's family. Jeev spun a convincing web of lies to hide his real identity. After they were finished with tea, Jeev said that he had a request to make.

'What is it?' Govind enquired.

'I imagine you must be in regular touch with your political contacts and friends in Delhi both in the ruling and opposition parties. Is it possible for you to ask them to

express their support for your cause through a resolution in the parliament?' Jeev enquired.

'Why?'

'To rattle the king and force him to give up his obduracy and also make his loyalists and the fence-sitters apprehensive of what Delhi may do next,' Jeev replied.

'Most of your leaders are aware of what I am up to,' Govind said. 'We are in constant dialogue on this subject. In fact, they keep urging me not to slow down our preparations for launching a mass movement.'

'That is not enough. You need to persuade them to pass a resolution in the parliament denouncing the king for his repressive regime and calling upon the Nepalese people to rise in revolt against him,' Jeev suggested.

'I will try, but what purpose will it serve?' Govind probed.

'It is essential to have adequate resources for any political movement to succeed. And, to make those resources available to you, the Agency will need to have a government in Delhi that is publicly committed to supporting your cause,' Jeev paused to gauge Govind's reaction to his offer of financial support.

'I will inform you through my cousin if I need your service money,' Govind said, sounding dismissive.

'We have done some spadework meanwhile to add momentum to your movement,' Jeev went on to press his point. 'Once you are ready to strike, give me a call. I will ignite the fire and thereafter it will be your turn to ensure that the flame spreads far and wide,' he explained.

'What kind of fire is this?' Govind enquired.

'Loosely speaking, it will be in the form of a sudden burst of violent protests, taking the king, the Royal Nepalese Army and his administration by complete surprise. I will

have it triggered, and then you can capitalize on it and turn it into a nationwide protest movement,' Jeev said.

At this point, Govind got up, went to the bedroom and returned with a piece of paper.

'This has my Delhi number and the address where I usually stay,' Govind said as he handed Jeev a slip of paper. 'Today is Friday. I should be there not this Sunday but the following one. Come and see me. We will have a lot to talk about,' he said, hinting that the meeting was over.

Taking his cue, Jeev stood up. 'Thank you for meeting me and allowing me to explain my role in achieving our common interests. Please rest assured that I will always be ready to provide every kind of monetary, political, moral and operational support to help you in your historic mission.'

'How close are you to your Chief and the prime minister?' Govind enquired in an effort to gauge the strength behind Jeev's claim of extending help.

'I am not close to either, but I can have your message sent to them and ensure that they support you,' Jeev stressed.

Govind nodded, apparently satisfied. 'Did you notice anyone watching you in the lobby?' he abruptly asked.

'No, but why do you ask?'

'The officers of your internal intelligence bureau generally keep a watch on my visitors. It is funny, but I mark it all the time. They are probably not aware that their home minister, foreign minister and prime minister are my old friends. They may report on your presence, giving away the secrecy of our meeting,' Govind speculated.

'I will manage that,' Jeev said and rang up the receptionist to ask her to locate his driver and have him call him. Ten minutes later, the driver was on the line. Jeev instructed him to return to the doctor's house and wait for him there. The

cousin then escorted him to the lobby. Jeev next called the airport to reserve two seats on the Indian Airlines flight to Delhi, but it was fully booked. He did not want to drive back to Lucknow as his back pain was threatening to lay him down. The cousin, who had overheard Jeev's fruitless call to the airport, offered to help. He called someone and within half an hour, secured two seats for Jeev on the afternoon flight to Delhi. Jeev thanked him profusely, saying that what he could not accomplish in India as an Indian, he had managed to do as a Nepalese citizen. He soon left for the doctor's house in a taxi to evade any watchers in the hotel premises. He picked up Maitri and their bags and headed to the airport in his official vehicle. He told the driver to return to Lucknow.

Jeevnathan reached Delhi at around 4.00 p.m. Two hours later, he was briefing Rajan about his meeting with Govind. Afterwards, Rajan spoke to his wife, telling her that he had invited Jeevnathan and his lovely daughter for dinner at the house that evening. As Naveen would explain to Jeev later, this was Rajan's way of honouring an officer's efforts.

At the Sunday meeting in Delhi, Govind sounded like a man possessed. He spoke excitedly of the stars favouring an imminent restoration of democracy in Nepal and why he could now clearly see the monarchy coming to an end within a matter of days. He gave Jeev a detailed recounting of his meeting with the Indian prime minister and the leader of the opposition, both of whom had given their positive and forthright offer of support. He mentioned that a statement from his Indian friends and parliamentarians backing the movement had already been finalized and was

likely to be released the following week. And Mukteshwar, the pragmatic, irrepressible Indian socialist leader, was all charged up to sound the bugle of revolt from Nepalese soil to launch the movement, he confided.

'Finally, everything is falling into place. I imagine the history of Nepal is about to be rewritten and when it happens, you will find a prominent place in its golden pages,' Jeev deliberately massaged Govind's ego, finding him keen to reveal more.

'I am not so sure, given how history can often be unkind in the hands of successors who nurse rival ambitions and profess different ideologies,' Govind remarked. 'Anyway, let's not look that far ahead for the time being. I have an important piece of information to share with you. When I went to Kathmandu after our last meeting, I noticed a remarkable change in the attitude of the communists. They no longer insisted on making Nepal a republic and seemed willing to accept a monarch with his wings clipped. I think it will be much easier now for me to coordinate the protests by the various groups and parties to mount the final offensive. But tell me honestly, did you speak to any of the leaders of the Communist Party of Nepal?' he asked.

'No, this is all due to your persuasive and forceful leadership and now that you have taken the reins of the movement in your hands, no one can stop the march of democracy,' Jeev said. 'Since you will be occupied with organizing the movement, will it still be possible for us to meet in the coming days?'

'You must come and see me whenever I am in Delhi. Apart from the fact that I enjoy talking to you, I may still need your advice. The mass upsurge is yet to kick off and who knows what turn it will take and when,' Govind said.

'It's so kind of you to say that. Did you receive the consignment that I sent through your cousin?' Jeev enquired.

'Yes. I hope he gave you a receipt for it,' Govind said.

Jeev nodded in confirmation and then took his leave.

Jeevnathan dispatched a detailed note on his second meeting with Govind to Naveen but heard nothing from headquarters in response. The earlier report on his first meeting had met with a similar fate. Naveen said that the reports were with the Chief, but he didn't know whether they had been trashed or were yet to be read.

Meanwhile, Jeev had two more meetings with Govind in Delhi. In the last meeting, Govind revealed the final plan for the protest marches and the terms of the broad agreement reached with the United Left Front and other political parties. He also told Jeev the date when Mukteshwar would land in Kathmandu to deliver his clarion call to the Nepalese people to launch a peaceful disobedience movement to force the king to restore democracy. He, however, sounded worried. His contacts in the Nepalese intelligence had confided that the king was determined to ruthlessly crush all forms of agitation against his regime. If that happened, Govind did not think the movement could be sustained beyond a week in the face of the inevitable large-scale arrests and heavy casualties in police retaliation. What also distressed him was Delhi's reluctance to officially warn the king of serious consequences should he use excessive force to crush the popular movement. He also suspected that the Maoists were buying time and that once democracy was restored, they would revive their armed struggle to ensure that the monarchy was consigned to history.

Jeev reported Govind's concerns to headquarters, but once again, heard nothing. He didn't know if anyone was reading his reports.

'At least I do,' Naveen said, allaying Jeev's misgivings during the latter's visit to headquarters. 'And why should it bother you so long as service money for this operation is being sent to you without any delay or cuts?'

'You're right.'

'By the way, the Chief was asking about the progress made on winding up the ESB. He's asked me to submit an interim report. Can you send me an update within a couple of days?' Naveen asked.

'No problem,' Jeev said.

'You know, your reports on Govind read more like fiction than a source report. They almost suggest that you're manufacturing the details to justify the relevance of the ESB. Maybe that's what provoked the Chief to suddenly enquire about the closure of the station.'

'Why doesn't he just issue an order setting a deadline and instruct all of us to disperse lock, stock and barrel? Why go through this charade of seeking weekly updates on what measures have been taken to close the bureau?' Jeev retorted. 'I must tell Rajan to stop wasting service money on my "stories",' he said in annoyance, reaching for the phone to call Rajan immediately.

'There is no point in ringing Rajan. He's in Colombo. I can't understand why you take everything so personally,' Naveen observed.

'Because I feel passionately about my work and don't like to be used. If the Chief is so determined to close the bureau, why did he ask for daily situation reports on the reserves of essential commodities during the blockade? And why

doesn't he tell me not to meet Govind and Bandicoot?' Jeev questioned.

'You have a point. I am also baffled. I really don't know what is going on,' Naveen said.

'Do you think Rajan and the Chief are not on the same page on running these operations and shutting down the ESB?' Jeev asked.

'It is unlikely. If that was the case, the Chief wouldn't sanction Govind's expenses so promptly,' Naveen said.

'Maybe I should continue running this operation and not bother the Chief with reports. He will either suspend further payments to Govind or ask for details on what is happening. But I am clear on one thing. I am not going to let Govind down. He was bitten once before by one of our chiefs. I don't want to be another Agency officer who betrays his trust,' Jeev asserted.

'But from where will you arrange the money to run this costly operation?' Naveen asked mischievously.

'Don't lose any sleep over it. I will float four bogus operations and claim money against them but actually pay Govind,' Jeev responded.

'I know you can go to any extent to protect your operations. But please don't stop submitting your reports. Just give me a few days. I will find out what happened to your previous reports,' Naveen said.

Strangely, headquarters' generosity ended with Govind. Whenever Jeev asked for funds for Bandicoot to be placed at his disposal so that payments could be made to him at short notice, Naveen would avoid committing them. Twice Jeev raised the issue of advances with Rajan and on

both occasions, he assured Jeev that they would be paid, but they never came. The Chief, in any case, was opposed to running Bandicoot. It was Rajan who was sustaining the operation by circumventing the normal route of funding. Under the circumstances, he didn't know what to do when he received a cable from Jogbani. Alok informed him that Bandicoot wished to meet him urgently, but this time in Rani village, at Tirtha's house. Though there was no mention of any request for money, Jeev did not want to travel empty-handed. He could beg and borrow money, but this arrangement was neither appropriate nor always feasible. He was also not comfortable meeting a fugitive from the law on Nepalese soil, particularly when the Chief had serious reservations about undertaking the operation. He called Rajan and guardedly apprised him of his predicament.

'I will have the money sent on time,' Rajan said. 'Whether you should meet the lion in his den is a decision that you have to take,' he added and hung up.

Jeev left the following day to meet Bandicoot. He arrived in Jogbani in the evening. At around 9.00 p.m., escorted by Alok, he made his way to the banks of the Parmar River, which had been reduced to a rivulet on the Indian side. They slowly negotiated the uneven, sandy riverbed in pitch darkness, finally reaching the opposite bank after almost half an hour. From there they walked for another twenty minutes on rutted lanes, taking care to move quietly and keep to the shadows. Finally, they arrived at Tirtha's house. It was a modest dwelling, built of mud and with an earthen tile roof. Tirtha made Jeev sit on a low wooden cot strung with jute strings woven in a beautiful pattern. It sagged in the middle but was still comfortable. He spread out a

bamboo mat for Alok. A kerosene lamp burnt dimly in the corner.

Kamal Aryal joined them after a few minutes. He shook Jeev's hand vigorously and thanked him for coming all the way from Delhi to see him. He dragged a wooden stool from the corner and sat on it, facing Jeev.

'I would have preferred to meet you in Jogbani, but I wanted to see whether you would run the risk of coming here or whether you believed only in others risking their lives for you,' he remarked light-heartedly.

'I guess I passed the test,' Jeev responded, smiling.

'Of course. I knew the very first day I met you that you were a brave man, just like one of us,' Aryal said and then asked Tirtha to serve dinner.

Sensing that Aryal did not want Tirtha to be privy to their discussion, Jeev also asked Alok to go out and help Tirtha.

'You may be interested in knowing what I have done with your money. Unlike your friends in the Nepali Congress, the Rashtriya Prajatantra Party and the Nepal Sadbhavana Party who spend money on building their personal fortunes, I have invested your money in preparing our cadre to organize uprisings in places where we are strong and where we can put up a tough fight against the administration,' Aryal said.

'I didn't come here to audit your expenditure,' Jeev interrupted.

'Good. I have already started working on your project. Two days before the protests explode, I will send you the exact date and locations of the agitations. As you suggested, I have also told the leaders of the Nepali Congress that the king as the nominal head of the state would be acceptable. It wasn't easy persuading some of the members of the

'We were asked to search all the houses in the area and this happens to be one of them,' Khem replied.

'Would you like to come inside and search?' asked Tirtha.

'No, that's fine. Let Mr Alok enjoy his dinner. I know his love for Nepalese food,' Khem said.

'But how does he know Tirtha?' another policeman enquired suspiciously.

'He teaches mathematics to Mr Alok's son,' Khem told his colleague.

Apparently satisfied, the policeman nodded and they all left.

Relieved, Tirtha returned to the room and let Aryal and Jeev out of their hiding place. He briefly recounted how the crisis had been averted. Aryal thanked Alok for his presence of mind. He then insisted that they all eat the dinner that had been so rudely interrupted. Tirtha brought out the food, but it was Aryal who served them soup in an earthen bowl followed by rice, meat and vegetables in plates made of leaves.

'Tirtha, thank you, the food was delicious,' said Jeev appreciatively.

'Sir, it's not me who deserves thanks,' Tirtha said. 'The leader insisted on cooking everything for you. That's why he came early.'

Aryal smiled. 'Years of living in the wilderness have taught me two good things. I have learnt to believe in destiny and cook for survival.'

After dinner, both Jeev and Alok made their careful way back. Once they were safely across the Parmar River, Jeev asked Alok about something that had struck him as odd.

'Tell me, Alok, why are there no women or children in Tirtha's house?'

'Sir, Tirtha is a bachelor. Serving the leader is all he cares about. His house functions as the secret meeting place for the armed cadres of the area. His neighbours, however, don't suspect a thing. They know him as a pleasant, simple, kind-hearted teacher.'

'Is Khem your source?' Jeev asked.

'Yes, sir,' Alok said.

Only thirty days were left until the final dismantling of the Eastern Service Bureau. All the logistics had been worked out. Only the sanction from headquarters for the projected expenditure was to be received. However, Jeev was in a dilemma. Almost all the sub-bureaus and employees had requested that the deadline be extended by one more month, citing operational and personal reasons that sounded very genuine. He knew that the Chief would dismiss their request, yet he didn't want to abdicate his responsibility towards his colleagues and their families without a fight. He decided to send a note to Naveen, arguing that granting a one-month extension wasn't unreasonable, especially if it benefitted the employees and helped conclude the closure on a less bitter note.

Later that evening, Rajan called.

'Your meetings have started stirring the situation. Things are moving fast and I want you now to walk ahead of the developments,' he said.

'Sir?' Jeev did not fully understand what Rajan was referring to.

'Come and see me in Delhi tomorrow. My secretary will make the necessary arrangements for your stay,' Rajan said

'Kanpur is not far. I want you to go there today and try to locate him. I am told there is a large Nepalese community in Varanasi. He may know people there who can help.'

'Sir, I used to know several Nepalese in Varanasi and shared reports from some of them, but headquarters did not find them useful. So I stopped meeting them. I can check if they are still around and whether they will be willing to assist us in this project,' Awasthy said.

'Start working on it immediately. You can begin by locating your contact in Kanpur. Then tomorrow, you can go to Varanasi, but tap only those who are virulently anti-king and habitual dissenters. And be discreet—don't share the real purpose behind distributing the weekly; first, sound out your contacts on whether anyone would be willing to launch a weekly in Nepali,' Jeev explained.

Later that night, Awasthy reported that his contact had sold his printing press and had opened a hardware shop. Nonetheless, he was interested in writing about the situation in Nepal and had offered to send articles on a regular basis. However, though he hated the means that the king was resorting to for suppressing the democratic movement, he had also expressed sympathy for the beleaguered monarch. Jeev decided not to use his services, fearing that he might betray them if the king was pushed beyond a point by agitators.

The following day, Awasthy left for Varanasi. Upon reaching, he headed straight for the neighbourhood where the majority of the Nepalese community lived. Luckily, most of his contacts still lived there. He first met Nischal, one of his closest assets who worked as a part-time journalist for a local vernacular daily and ran a provisions store that

was very popular in his community. Contrary to Jeev's advice, Awasthy confided the objective of the project to Nischal. The latter responded positively. He told Awasthy that he would host a dinner that night at his house where Awasthy could meet people from diverse fields and select the right people for his project.

The dinner went well. Nischal had invited a large number of his Nepalese friends, coming from almost all walks of life. As the evening progressed, he introduced Awasthy to a young and fiery school teacher, a part-time professor, a bookshop owner, a social activist known to be a vocal critic of the king and three stringers who contributed regularly to Nepalese national dailies on developments in India. Without giving too much away, Awasthy sounded them out on contributing articles on the situation in Nepal. To his relief, they were excited by the prospect of helping to spread awareness on the true intent of the king and his doings. Only the brooding professor was sceptical. He pointed out that it would be difficult to turn people in rural and semi-urban areas against the king, whom they saw as an incarnation of Lord Vishnu. He did not think anyone would risk reading material against the king, however juicy or informed it may be. Awasthy, he said, was probably not aware of how timid the Nepalese were and how brutal the police, intelligence and armed forces could be. Awasthy refrained from commenting on his observations, merely saying that he would soon be in touch with more details and requested them, in the meantime, to start writing on the developments in Nepal.

The following morning, Nischal took Awasthy to meet Shankar Thapa, a former commissioner of the Gandaki zone

in Nepal. He had been removed from the king's service for his alleged sympathy for the protesters. Fearing imminent imprisonment on trumped-up charges, Thapa had fled to Varanasi some six months ago.

Awasthy's meeting with Thapa turned out to be largely one-sided. Intimidated by Thapa's authoritative manner, his scholarship, and his in-depth knowledge of the political situation in his country, Awasthy remained silent for the most part. In any event, Thapa did not leave him much room to speak, as he lectured Awasthy on the state of anarchy and poverty in Nepal, blaming Delhi's spineless leadership for aiding the king's belligerence and his increasing proximity to China. He claimed that India had lost a great opportunity to squeeze the king dry when it had imposed the economic blockade. That was the time, he argued, when India could have wrested every possible concession and delivered a functional democracy to Nepal in return. He also found fault with India's handling of the Maoists and its unilateral support to the Nepalese Congress.

Finally, having had enough of Thapa's agitated monologue, Awasthy interrupted.

'Will it be possible for you to meet my boss?' he asked.

'Who is he?'

'He is your counterpart in Lucknow. Actually, it is on his specific direction that I am here. He asked me to enquire about your welfare and find out whether the police are harassing you,' Awasthy quickly improvised.

'Does he know me?'

'He may not know you personally, but he is aware of your background and why you fled your country to live here,' Awasthy replied.

'When can I meet him?'

'Any time that suits you,' Nischal intervened, taking over the discussion. 'You will find him extremely well informed on Nepal. I met him briefly, but it is better if he meets someone at your level. He can be of great help to our community in solving our day-to-day problems with the civil administration,' Nischal urged.

'Can he join me for dinner tomorrow at my residence?' Thapa asked.

'Yes, I'm sure he will be able to,' Awasthy replied.

'Is he an intelligence officer?' Thapa suddenly enquired.

'Yes,' Awasthy said after a brief pause.

'So, he is not exactly my counterpart.'

'That's right. Would you still like to have him over for dinner?' Awasthy enquired with a straight face.

Thapa looked thoughtful before finally agreeing. 'Yes. I'd like to at least hear what he has to say.'

Dinner was a lavish spread of Nepali cuisine. Mrs Thapa briefly appeared, exchanged pleasantries and withdrew, hoping that Jeev would enjoy the food. The conversation was deliberately general, Jeev and Thapa using the opportunity to size up one another. After dinner, Thapa led Jeev to his study. Awasthy and Nischal moved to the living room. Jeev wasted no time in explaining the purpose of his visit and sought Thapa's advice on how to go about it. Thapa was struck by Jeev's candour.

'I don't think you will achieve anything by distributing a weekly tabloid,' Thapa opined. 'A large percentage of the rural population is illiterate and among those who can read,

few will have the courage to rise up against the king. They may read the weekly and gossip about its contents behind closed doors but that is where their response will end. You are actually targeting the wrong people. They are weak and helpless and are resigned to living under the king's subjugation. For generations they have treated him as the seventh avatar of Lord Vishnu and they genuinely believe that God will punish them if they protest against his rule,' he explained.

'I am not concerned with what they do or don't do. Nor is it my brief to assess the utility of this exercise. I simply want a weekly to be published on the lines that I mentioned to you,' Jeev responded curtly.

'Since you insist, I will give it a try. What I can do is to regularly contribute articles and translate material provided by you, but that won't be enough. You will have to rope in at least a dozen reporters, an able editor and a publisher, apart from distributers within Nepal,' Thapa said.

'Given your administrative experience, I would like you to coordinate the pooling of reports from various sources, their editing, proofreading and printing. Awasthy has a list of people who have volunteered to write for the magazine. They are all from Nepal, but are now living in Varanasi, pursuing various professions. Awasthy will arrange for you to meet with them. You can guide them on what to write and how. They will file their reports under pseudonyms so that their family members and relatives in Nepal are protected from possible reprisals from the king's goons. After the weeklies are published, Awasthy will handle their distribution,' Jeev explained.

'How do I contact you if I have any questions?' Thapa asked.

'Awasthy can take care of all your requirements and doubts. I travel a lot and with the communication network being what it is, it will be difficult for you to get in touch with me when you really need to talk. That is why I have asked Awasthy to remain in constant touch with you,' Jeev said.

'Let's hope it works out as you have envisioned. I seldom take up projects without careful planning and in ugly haste. I hope the weekly doesn't turn out to be a third-rate rag. It won't serve your purpose if people start suspecting that an Indian intelligence agency is orchestrating a crude propaganda war,' Thapa remarked.

'That is precisely why I came to you,' Jeev said. 'With your years of experience, I can't see you failing in this enterprise. I am also told you had a two-year stint with the *Kathmandu Post* and occasionally wrote for the weekly *Jan Aastha*. In fact, that was what prompted me to approach you.'

'You seem to know a lot about my background,' Thapa smiled.

'Only what is relevant to the project,' Jeev said. 'I wish I had been given more time to bring out a high-quality publication. Since that luxury is not available, we have to put out the first issue within a fortnight. Don't worry about money. Awasthy will take care of that. I will send you the material for the first print of the weekly by tomorrow. It will help you understand how news and articles are written for subverting people's loyalty to an oppressive regime. You can show it to other contributors as well so they can tailor their articles accordingly,' he added.

Thapa found Jeevnathan to be overbearing but opted to play along for the time being.

'I have a cousin working in a very senior position in the Nepalese intelligence,' he claimed, subtly hinting to Jeev that he was aware of how intelligence officers operated. 'If you want, I can put you in touch with him.'

'We can discuss that on another day. For the present, the weekly is my topmost priority,' Jeev did not let Thapa digress from the main issue.

Business concluded, Jeev thanked his host for the dinner and for his help, and handed him a packet. 'This has a small gift for Mrs Thapa. My wife has sent it for her. I hope she likes it,' he said.

Shortly after, Jeev, Awasthy and Nischal left.

Thapa christened the twenty-page weekly *Bihane*. It came out two days earlier than the date stipulated by Rajan. It carried news, features and articles, highlighting police atrocities, corruption in the Royal Nepalese Army and the lavish lifestyle of the king. It also featured a cartoon showing the king's head bending backward under the weight of his sins. Thapa's editorial was crisp and trenchant. It indicted the king severely for his administrative blunders, which, among other things, had led to increasing poverty among the people.

The drill for distributing the weekly also ran smoothly. After printing, the magazines were stored in Nischal's house, from where they were dispatched to Lucknow, and from there to selected officers in sub-bureaus located along the border. The Nepalese couriers picked up their respective quota of weeklies during the night and had them distributed through secure hands to public places, houses of officials, shops and restaurants. It was distributed for free.

The impact of *Bihane* was decisive. Such was the demand that the number of copies printed had to be trebled. The contents fuelled animated discussions behind closed doors and readers particularly looked forward to the cartoon lampooning the king, his family members, his political minions and the infighting among the opposition parties. The weekly soon caught the attention of bewildered Nepalese officials. Police raided suspected distribution points, forcing circulation to be more secretive and widely awaited. Intelligence agencies were directed to identify the source of the publication. They questioned the usual suspects and their contacts, but no one volunteered any information.

One day, Jeev received in the mail a copy of the weekly from Rajan. On a slip stapled to the magazine he had written: *Sent by a journalist friend from Kathmandu.*

With the weekly running successfully and with no news from either Govind or Aryal, Jeev had plenty of time to finalize the closure of the Eastern Service Bureau. He sent out a detailed plan of withdrawal of men and material to all employees and asked them to be ready to move at short notice and forwarded a copy to Naveen.

He next decided to get in touch with Vidyadhar Banerjee. With Rao's assistance and after a few initial technical hiccups, Jeev managed to get through to him.

'Any news from Govind?' he asked.

'No, sir. But his cousin is here, sitting in the adjoining room. I had called him to receive the last consignment of the service money,' Vidyadhar reported.

'Did he say anything about our next meeting?' Jeev enquired.

'No, sir, but he did say that Govind would meet you only after the mission was accomplished, which his cousin believes is imminent,' Vidyadhar said.

'That's fine with me,' Jeev said.

'Sir, have I lived up to your expectations?' Vidyadhar asked suddenly.

'Yes, you have. I always knew you had the potential to produce wonders,' Jeev assured him before hanging up.

He next contacted Alok. It took nearly an hour for the operator to establish the link with the Jogbani sub-bureau.

'Did your friend get back to you after receiving the second instalment?' Jeev asked as soon as Alok came on the line.

'No, sir. But I met Tirtha recently. He told me that Bandicoot has gone underground and is unlikely to surface in the near future. He sent a message for you through Tirtha; he urgently needs two more consignments of service money. I sent you his request via cable about an hour ago,' he added.

'I have a contact in Patna and will send you his contact details. Go to him after two days to collect the money. Give my reference,' Jeev instructed him.

A week later, Jeev woke up early as usual, though it was Sunday. Manini was barely awake when he wished her a happy birthday and a long life. As she rolled over to face him with her eyes half-closed, Jeev repeated his wishes.

'Thanks, but don't overdo it,' she said and fell asleep again.

Used to her barbs, he went to the living room, collected the newspapers and settled down to read. He had just been served his tea when the phone rang. Manini called out loudly from the bedroom, asking him to answer it. By the

time he reached it, the phone stopped ringing. He drew back the curtains, allowing the sunlight to invade the room and settled back into his easy chair. He resumed reading the newspaper when the phone rang again. This time he answered it before it got disconnected. The operator informed him that a call from Delhi was being put through. It was the Chief.

'Something serious is brewing in the neighbourhood and I want you to go there immediately,' he growled. 'The order for your transfer is on the way and I expect you to join your new assignment within a fortnight,' he added and then hung up.

Jeev was baffled by the Chief's cryptic instructions. He had no idea where he had to go or what he was required to do. He promptly booked a lightning call to Rajan. Ten minutes later, he got through and reported verbatim what the Chief had just told him. Rajan told him not to worry.

'Your transfer was decided last evening,' he informed him. 'I actually pushed the Chief to select you for this job. Take a flight to Delhi and meet me in the office before 7.00 p.m. I will explain everything,' he said and dropped the phone.

'When do we start packing for the next station?' Manini asked. Apparently, she had overheard his conversation with Rajan.

'I will know that only after I meet Rajan in Delhi today,' Jeev said.

'I didn't know you were such a lightweight that they could toss you around with such ease,' she remarked.

'Mani, this bureau is going to be closed down in three to four weeks. So how does it matter whether I leave now

or after a month? I thought you would be happy that they need me desperately to handle a crisis,' Jeev said.

'I don't know when you will stop living under this belief in your self-importance. Actually, your Agency finds it convenient to use you in their scheme of things,' Manini averred.

Jeev ignored her remarks and booked his flight to Delhi.

His meeting with Rajan left him with mixed feelings. The latter explained the nature of his assignment and told him where he was going to be located. Jeev wasn't sure what to make of this unexpected development. He speculated that either they had entrusted him with the new job after observing his handling of a few operations over the last couple of months. Or they had decided to transfer him to ensure that the Eastern Service Bureau was wound up smoothly. Perhaps the Chief was fed up with his repeated requests to extend the deadline, he speculated.

'Sir, I don't know what to think, but why select someone who has not even completed his mandatory tenure in India for an overseas assignment?' he enquired.

'Because that someone is a good operator and can take risks,' Rajan said with a smile.

'But sir, who will handle Govind, Bandicoot and *Bihane*?'

'That should no longer be your worry,' Rajan said as he stood up. 'The Chief is waiting for you. I suggest you simply listen to what he has to say,' Rajan advised him in conclusion.

Jeev's meeting with the Chief was short. The latter said nothing about the closure of the bureau, Govind, Bandicoot or *Bihane* and spoke only about the operational challenges

that Jeev would be facing in his new assignment. Jeev merely listened.

That evening, Rajan took Jeev out for dinner. Finding him relaxed and animated, Jeev sensed it was an opportune time to question him on the fate of his current operations.

'Sir, you didn't tell me who will be running Govind and Aryal and supervising Thapa's work. We have invested so much in these assets and now when they are fully primed to launch the movement, you are transferring me,' he said.

'You have unleashed the beast, Jeev. It's not going to stop until the monarchy is pulled down. Even if we try to contain it, we won't succeed,' Rajan chuckled.

'And what about the decision to close the ESB?'

'You have played foul,' Rajan said with a straight face. 'Who in his right mind will now even talk about winding up the bureau when so many high-grade operations are underway? Actually, we seriously started having a rethink after you met Raghupati. Thereafter we even stopped mentioning the subject,' he said with a huge smile.

'But then why is the Chief hostile towards me?'

'He envies you as an operator and cannot stomach your aloof style of running things. In any case, he is retiring next month. He is not even eligible to write your confidential report since you have worked under him for less than six months,' Rajan said.

Back in Lucknow, Jeev told Manini about his meetings with the Chief and Rajan. But she was not impressed.

'I have a better sense of reading the situation,' she opined. 'Since no one would have opted to go to that wretched place, they decided to banish you there. Anyway, since I have no choice, I will have to follow you wherever you

go as an obedient housewife. But I won't let Adya's studies suffer in that primitive place. She stays in India.'

'I will go by your decision.'

Later in the day, Jeev sent a brief message to the officers in charge of all sub-bureaus. It read:

'The ESB is not being disbanded and will continue to function as before. This has been possible because the station's performance has improved dramatically during the last twelve weeks. I must commend in particular three sub-bureaus that produced wonders in terms of tapping high-grade sources and running them productively. However, unlike all of you, I am not so lucky. I have been posted out and asked to leave the station within a week. In my absence, deputy Awasthy will look after my work.'

The following day, Jeevnathan received three cables. Bipin Verma wrote that Raghupati wanted to know if he could invite Jeev for his swearing-in ceremony as a cabinet minister at the Raj Bhavan in Lucknow. Vidyadhar Banerjee expressed dismay over Jeev's sudden exit in the middle of a very critical operation and insisted that he was not capable of handling such a high-grade source. Alok Raut conveyed that Bandicoot had asked for one last meeting with Jeev before triggering violent protests. Jeev read the cables over and over again and then replied cryptically to all three:

'Consider that I do not exist and then respond to the situation accordingly.'

Waiting at the Indira Gandhi International Airport in Delhi to board the Indian Airlines flight to his new destination, Jeevnathan picked up a copy of *The Times of India* and started glancing through it. A small news item on the third page caught his attention. In Rolpa, Rukum and Jajarkot in Nepal, violence had suddenly erupted over the refusal of the police to release Maoist detainees and it had quickly spread to several places in nine other districts. Jeev was overcome with a surge of emotion and gratitude. Bandicoot had kept his promise. The people's revolution, which he had so passionately advocated, had begun. And the democracy that Govind was determined to restore was only half a step away from becoming a reality.

Postscript

Raghupati served as minister for two terms in the government of Uttar Pradesh. He never called Jeevnathan or met him. Democracy was restored in Nepal and the king was reduced to being a ceremonial head in the new government. Back with a bang on the centre stage of politics in Nepal, Govind and Bandicoot tried to track down 'Karthik Sharma' (Jeevnathan's nom-de-plume) for years but had no luck. Thapa returned to Kathmandu to take up an important ambassadorial assignment in Europe. Although never particularly fond of Jeevnathan, he nonetheless wanted to personally express his gratitude to the man who had met all his financial requirements without questioning him and had also ensured that no one harassed him during his exile. When pressed repeatedly, Awasthy told him that Jeevnathan

had left Lucknow, but nobody knew where he had gone. Thapa, however, refused to believe the lie. Bipin, Vidyadhar and Alok, the three field operatives who had worked closely with Jeevnathan, were sent in due course to take up various assignments in India and abroad. Never again did they serve under Jeevnathan or run into him even accidentally.